I0676877

Wingman by Catherine King: A military experiment gave Sam wings. Now he has the pleasure of flight... and unexpected other pleasures as well.

Valkyrie's Child by Ann Gimpel: The Elder Council stripped Astyr's wings from her, for the crime of loving the wolfish hunter in the hills.

Underneath It All by Kailin Morgan: Below the tube station, a man with tattered white wings is bound by chains with no locks.

Devilish Trick by L.D. Durham: When an angel makes a bargain with a demon, he risks corruption and damnation for an evening of lust.

Falling into Her Arms by Laylah Hunter: Even an angel cannot withstand the will of Heaven for long, but Ambriel clings to the memory of her lover.

Icarus Bleeds by Annabeth Leong: In a world where any body modification is available for a price, Icarus sells all he has--his body--to get wings.

Elf Esteem by Nobilis Reed: Domination is a matter of attitude and spirit, not size.

If you enjoy this collection, you can sign up for a free membership at
ForbiddenFiction.com and discuss it with other readers
and the authors at the *Taking Flight* story page
at http://forbiddenfiction.com/library/collection/SPC-1.100004.

We do our best to proof all our work, but if you spot a text error we missed,
please let us know via our website Contact Form
at http://forbiddenfiction.com/contact.

Also recommended...

You may also enjoy these other ForbiddenFiction special collections:

Wicked Fairy Tales
An anthology of bedtime stories for adults!

Just what kind of happy goes into "happily ever after?" Being a real boy means having boy parts, and being eaten by someone big and bad doesn't mean quite the same thing it once did.

Ever wonder what mermaids do with the swimmers they seduce? Or why a dragon might prefer a castle-guarded princess to a nice, easy field of sheep? What if your fairy godmother wasn't circumspect in what wishes could be granted, or if that dainty little fairy had a much bigger appetite than one might guess?

http://forbiddenfiction.com/library/story/SPC-1.100002

Coming Soon... Bi Magic: Best Bisexual Fantasy
High fantasy, high passions: sorcerers and royalty have never been bound by common relationship roles.
- To Market by Elizabeth Schechter: Meet the fae creature who delights in human beauty in any form.
- Snake & Lyre by Annabeth Leong: The virgin maid loves her fiance... but is enthralled by the ladies of the underworld.
- The Thief's Dungeon by Madeleine Swann: She may lust after her jailer, but he's not the first to sample her charms.

... and six more!

http://forbiddenfiction.com/library/story/SPC-1.100005

Taking Flight

a ForbiddenFiction Special Collection

edited by D.M. Atkins

ForbiddenFiction
www.forbiddenfiction.com

an imprint of

Fantastic Fiction Publishing
www.fantasticfictionpub.com

TAKING FLIGHT
A Forbidden Fiction book

Fantastic Fiction Publishing
Hayward, California

© D.M. Atkins, 2014

All rights reserved. No part of this work may be used or reproduced in any manner whatsoever without permission from the publisher, except as allowed by fair use. For more information, contact publisher@ forbiddenfiction.com.

CREDITS
Editors: D.M. Atkins, Rylan Hunter, Lon Sarver
Cover Design: Siolnatine
Cover Photo: Sanches1980 at Dreamstime
Internal cover art: Siolnatine; Ekhphoto, Marcinski and Curaphotography, Macmoss, Mocker and SpinningAngel, Mimagephotography at Dreamstime
Internal cover design: D.M. Atkins and Siolnatine
Production Editor: Erika L Firanc
Proofreading: Kailin Morgan, XochitLina, Jae Knight, Todd Michaels

SKU: SPC-100004-02 FFP
ISBN: 978-1-62234-172-6

Published in the United States of America

DISCLAIMER

This book is a work of fiction which contains explicit erotic content; it is intended for mature readers. Do not read this if it's not legal for you.

All the characters, locations and events herein are fictional. While elements of existing locations or historical characters or events may be used fictitiously, any resemblance to actual people, places or events is coincidental.

This book depicts depicts fictional BDSM; it is not intended to be used as an instruction manual. It contains descriptions of erotic acts that may be immoral, illegal, or unsafe. The characters are not models for the Safe, Sane and Consensual forms embraced by most current practitioners of BDSM. The authors take license with the use of BDSM for dramatic effect. Do not take the events in this story as proof of the plausibility or safety of any particular practice.

To Maya Angelou, whose inspirational work
gave us flights of hope and helped provide
the courage to follow our passions.

Contents

Wingman

Katherine King

Catherine King has written erotic fiction, both original and fan works, for over a decade, and specializes in erotica with sci-fi or historical themes. She is especially interested in exploring the erotic possibilities of alien cultures, body transformation, and artificial intelligence in her work. When she's not writing, Catherine works for a local charity in northern Thailand, and can usually be found wobbling her way from street market to street market on her beloved hand-me-down red motorcycle.

Chapter 1
Metamorphosis

Sam Wilson wriggled experimentally, testing the give in the two leather straps that crossed his bare chest and thighs.

Conclusion: There wasn't much.

The straps weren't quite biting into him—not yet—but when he moved, they tightened uncomfortably. The padded cuffs around his wrists and ankles were a little more forgiving, allowing him to lift his limbs slightly; however, the heavy chains attaching the cuffs to the cold steel table only gave him a few inches of movement in any direction. The worst part was the band of leather across his forehead, preventing him from looking around the room. All he could see were the dingy grey outlines of ventilation pipes, winding their way across the ceiling far above. The ceiling itself was lost in the darkness beyond.

Sam could feel a cold sweat starting on his forehead, seeping under the band and making the slick leather chafe against his skin. The irritation, just this side of pain, made him wince and squirm harder; the shift caused the strap across his torso to catch, the metal buckle abruptly cutting into his skin. A numbness in his fingertips was the first sign of the oncoming panic, and Sam bit down on a whimper.

Unacceptable, Wilson. His trainer's voice always filtered into his head at times like these. Not his old drill sergeant from his army days, but his trainer from the agency who had taken them in, a small cadre of aimless ex-soldiers, and shaped them into what they were now. He could still imagine her hissing in his ear. *Fear is failure. Fear will get you killed. You are fearless, or you are nothing.*

Eyes closed, Sam held his breath, the focus of his mind telescoping inward. He waited until there was a tiny ache in his chest, then slowly exhaled, feeling the tight knot dissolve. Inhale again, hold it to the point of pain, and then let it go. The small fact that he could control the tightness in his chest, creating it and then making it go away, helped make the tightness of his bonds seem less overwhelming.

Easy, Wilson. That thought was in his own voice. *And remember that you asked for this.*

The corners of Sam's mouth turned up in a shaky smile.

It had started a few days earlier, when a voice from the other end of the hallway had called after him, "Wilson, hold up a second."

Sam had turned, surprised. The commander of Covert Ops rarely spoke to his operatives directly; Sam hadn't even been sure that the man knew his name before this. "Yessir?"

The commander had looked him up and down appraisingly. "Wilson, you've been with us a while, haven't you?"

"Five years, sir."

"Five years, hmm. And are you happy?"

Sam had waffled over the answer for a second. *Getting a bit metaphysical today, aren't we, sir?* had warred in his head with the equally inappropriate, *Yes, sir, frontline grunt for a shadowy extra-governmental agency is exactly the job I picked out back at Career Day in high school,* but he'd managed a bland, "Can't complain, sir. The agency's been good to me all this time."

"Still, plugging away in the field for five years, and you're still only a Level 3, isn't that right? That's got to be frustrating."

It hadn't been a question, so Sam hadn't treated it as one. Instead, he'd stood in parade rest, his half-lidded eyes watching the commander's smile.

After waiting expectantly for a moment, the commander had shrugged. "Look, I'll come to the point. The kooks down in Science Division have a new serum. They're looking for some poor chump to test it out on."

Sam had tilted his head. "Well, honestly, sir, I may not have had a promotion in a while, but I wouldn't say it's left me feeling *suicidal.*"

The smile had narrowed, until it showed only the tips of the commander's teeth. "If it takes—and if you survive it—we're talking about bumping you up a couple of grades. Using you in the special-ised missions."

Despite himself, Sam had leaned forward.

The commander had noticed it, too. Smirking, he'd added, "You'll be our new secret weapon, Wilson."

"Sir, if I might ask—what does the serum *do*?"

"Eh, it reconfigures your genetic thingamabobs."

That hadn't sounded particularly reassuring.

"I think *splicing* is involved."

That had sounded worse.

"Look, just get the kooks to explain it to you. Sub-level Eleven; they're expecting you. That is, if you agree?"

Sam had opened his mouth to reply, when he'd heard someone shout his name.

"Sam, if you're going to—oh." Jonathan Harris had come skidding to a stop next to Sam, and had given a lazy salute. "Sir."

The commander had barely spared him a glance; instead, he'd nodded to Sam. "Think it over. You can still say no, once you've talked to Science Division. But, Wilson? I wouldn't pass this opportunity up lightly if I were you." He'd turned to frown at Jon, then. "What about you, Harris? Are you happy in your current position?"

"It's everything I've dreamed of ever since I was a tiny child," Jon had deadpanned. The commander had pursed his lips, but had said nothing more, walking off to leave the two alone.

"You really shouldn't do that, you know. One day, he's actually going to stop putting up with it," Sam had murmured, a faint smile playing over his lips. Jon had waved him off.

"Never mind that. Science Division? What was that about?"

Sam had explained the choice to him, watching his thoughtful frown deepen. When Sam was finished, Jon had shuddered.

"Yeah, I've heard of Command pulling this before. Promotions, glory, place in the history books—if anything the agency ever did was printable, which, of course, it isn't. All in exchange for letting them slice and dice you into the ultimate weapon. Of course, you'd have to be bugfuck to even consider it."

Sam had taken a deep breath.

"Oh, Christ, you're considering it."

"I'm—I'm playing with the idea. Of at least hearing them out. No harm in that, right?"

Jon had flung an arm around Sam's shoulders, pulling him close. Sam had stifled a groan. Jon being affectionate was nothing new, and it wasn't as if Sam was always above enjoying his best friend's platonic touches for less-than-strictly-platonic reasons. The problem was, it was damned distracting, especially when Sam needed to think. Jon's messy shock of black hair had brushed teasingly against his cheek, and long, clever fingers that were as elegant and precise priming a detonator as they were on Sam's skin had danced over his arm, and finally curled around his shoulder.

"You don't need any fucking serum, buddy. You're a damn good agent, you know that, right? Promotion or no promotion, they can't take that away from you. Why would you want to go fucking up your DNA just to get a pat on the head from the commander?"

Easy for you to say, Sam had thought, his brown eyes meeting Jon's wide grey ones sidelong. *Jon the tech guy. Jon the genius. Jon who could blow up the entire headquarters and dance around naked in the ashes, and they still wouldn't be able to fire you, because no one else can do what you do. I don't mind my job, but I'm a grunt—always have been. I'm not like you. If I got killed tomorrow, they could replace me before I was cold.*

I just… I want to be more than that.

After a long moment, he'd shrugged. "Sounds interesting, is all. I've been pretty bored in the field, lately. I could use something to shake things up. Besides"—and he'd lifted a hand to ruffle the already irredeemable bird's nest that was Jon's hair—"how often does someone offer you the chance to get superpowers, hmm?"

"Around here? Every other week." Jon had folded his arms across his chest. "Sam, folks who go down to Science Division come back with three heads. Or they don't come back at all."

"Oh, come on, that was once. And Smith was able to get the extra heads removed."

"Yeah, it's the *not come back at all* part I'm a little more concerned about."

"I'm just going to talk to them." And Sam had grinned, turning and looking into those wide, nervous eyes. "Fuck—if I'd wanted to stay safe all the time, I never would have signed up to this outfit in the first place."

The words felt bright and hollow in his memory as Sam stared up at the pipes, and the blackness surrounding them.

"Ah, good. I see my assistants have thoroughly prepared you, Agent Wilson."

The voice was a low, heady purr, too close to his ear for comfort. Slender fingers ghosted over Sam's face, checking his pupils, minutely adjusting the fit of the leather strap across his forehead. Sam could sense, more than see, an intense light switch on, just at the corner of his vision, but the wider room remained dark.

Something flickered in the light. A thin flare, resolving itself into the shining point of a needle. Sam relaxed, thinking that at least they were going to put him under first.

He was wrong. A moment later, Sam screamed.

Even after five years with the agency, it had taken Sam a depressingly long time to *find* Science Division. He'd identified the general area of Sub-level Eleven easily—the muffled bangs and squawks would have been a dead giveaway, even without the smell—but the actual door had turned out to be lurking down a blind alley, past a sign that said NO ENTRY and bore illustrations of stick figures keeling over in hideous ways to back it up.

The main laboratory had been occupied only by a single lab-coated man, who'd been pouring something purple and shimmering into a test tube. Sam had hovered in the doorway for almost a minute, unsure whether he should disturb the process. Instead, he'd watched the scientist work. Something about the man's bearing and his perfectly sculpted red hair had made him look like he'd be more at home propping up a country club bar than conducting experiments. Nevertheless, it had been impossible to mistake the avid gleam in his sharp blue eyes as he'd watched the liquid in the tube swirl and shift.

Delicate fingers, that had instantly reminded Sam of Jon's, had curled almost possessively around the test tube, and the scientist's wide, sensitive mouth had curved up at one corner as the liquid had turned the colour of blood.

Putting the tube down, the scientist had spotted Sam out of the corner of his eye and jumped. Sam had started to apologise for sneaking up on him, but the man had smirked, reaching up to run a hand over his hair, as if brushing a non-existent stray strand back into place. "My, you're light on your feet. Covert Ops, am I right?" His voice was smooth, and had lingered over the words with a certain relish. "You must be Agent Wilson. Please, call me Doctor."

Sam had waited politely, until he'd realised that was the end of the sentence, and a name was not forthcoming. Doctor had smiled wider as he'd taken Sam's hand in a firm handshake. The scientist's fingers had been smooth and surprisingly warm against his own.

"Basically," Doctor had told him, ushering Sam into an inner office, "the serum allows us to isolate specific traits from other animal species, and combine them with a human form." Those elegant hands had firmly pushed the agent down into a chair. "We're hoping to expand to non-animal species eventually—personally, I think there's great potential in field agents who would be able to manufacture their own food through photosynthesis—" At Sam's alarmed look, he had broken off and laughed—a little self-conscious, but throaty and rather appealing. "Never mind. That's only a flight of fancy of mine. Your commander is much more interested in the *classics*."

Sam had sat rigidly at attention as Doctor had dimmed the lights and toggled a few keys on a laptop, triggering a holographic display in front of them. "So… what exactly are we talking about here, Doctor?" he'd asked, laughing nervously. "Animal traits… you mean you want to give me a tail, or something? Turn me into a werewolf?"

There had been a brief moment of silence, and then those warm hands had settled on his shoulders again, and stayed. "Oh, no," Doctor had breathed. "Nothing that crude, Agent Wilson. No, we have something much more… *spectacular* in mind for you."

And he had brought up an image on the display.

Sam's mouth had gone dry. Thoughts of mystery drugs, of side effects, of staggering monstrosities in agony and of body bags quietly hauled out of the labs at night had flown across his mind. He'd known it was insane, known he should ask a thousand more questions.

But he'd swallowed, hard, his eyes fixed on the image. "All right," he'd whispered.

Those words were echoing in his head now, as he thrashed on the medical table. He could feel the serum creeping through him; it was viscous and cold, cold enough to burn, like razors dragging inside his veins. The worst part wasn't even the pain, but the fact that there was no way he could twist to get away from it. In the back of his mind, he was dimly glad he'd been strapped down. Otherwise, he might have been tearing at his arms, just trying to rip the torturous feeling *out*.

Doctor's fingertips stroked over Sam's cheek, which was soaked with sweat, despite the cold. "Shhh." Sam tried to focus on those minuscule points of heat, instead of the awful cold. Slowly — so slowly — the pain eased, as the cold gradually spread through every inch of his body; his fingers and feet were starting to numb, but now that the serum seemed to be distributed in his blood, it no longer chafed as it crawled through his veins. Doctor was murmuring something soft, but whether it was encouragement for Sam, or simply a running commentary for the many cameras recording the process, Sam couldn't tell. The pain had exhausted him, and the numbness was starting to make him feel sleepy…

"Very good, Agent," Doctor said close to his ear. "*Very* good. You're doing well. Now, we should have a good fifteen minutes' respite be —"

He never got the chance to finish the sentence. Sam bucked in his restraints and screamed as the skin of his back abruptly pulled tight. To his horror, he could feel it start to rip. Doctor's fingers were frantic, undoing the strap across his forehead, then the one at his chest, as Sam bit down hard on his lower lip, trying to muffle his frightened yell. As soon as the second strap was off, Sam bolted upright as far as the cuffs would allow, just as the skin of his back burst fully open, like overripe fruit.

He was in agony, fighting back tears; he could feel blood running hot down the ruins of his back to pool under his hips. Doctor was making distracted shushing noises as he raced around, punching in codes to the dozen monitors that were now blaring frantic alarms. What was happening had clearly come too soon. Another wave of pain went through him, and Sam felt like he was going to be sick. Clenching his teeth and breathing raggedly, he shut his eyes, wondering whether he was about to die.

And then something new happened. Not pain—a bizarre feeling, almost a relief, like a kink in a muscle suddenly loosening, right between his shoulder blades. With a wet crackle, some part of his back was folding outwards. Sam fell silent, in spite of the anguish. That caught Doctor's attention. A second later, the scientist was next to him, gently wiping at Sam's back with a cool cloth that stank of something astringent. It stung, and Sam hissed in a breath. Doctor's free hand came to rest on Sam's arm, just above his cuffed wrist.

"Easy, now. Just something to prevent infection. There seems to have been quite a bit of damage to the muscular structure—more than we anticipated." Even though the liquid burned, the motion was kind of soothing. "That happened a lot faster than we were ready for." He was frowning, but not in remorse; it was more of a pout, as if the failure of the experiment to progress exactly as planned was a personal affront. "Now, let's see here."

Sam was curled forward, shaking, weathering the spasms of pain as they washed over him. He didn't move when Doctor stopped wiping down his back, but the scientist's next motion drew a gasp from him. Doctor was very carefully tugging at his back — at the part that he could now feel jutting out at an unnerving angle. The damp sounds it made were faintly sickening, but the pull felt *wonderful*, like a massage. Sam let out a low groan, as what felt like an entire portion of his back came undone, slithering loose and flopping down onto the table with a squelch.

Sam carefully twisted around, taking in the raw, bloodied thing lying next to him. "Is… is that really…"

"Oh, *yes*." Doctor's smile could not have been smugger if he'd tried. "Hold on a moment." Some more delicate manoeuvring, Doctor's fingers digging in here and there—even that felt perversely good—and another blood-slick appendage came free on the other side and unfurled, brushing his arm on the way down. It was soft.

Sam could almost forget the slowly-dissipating ache as he watched Doctor's fingers work over the first of the appendages, meticulously wiping away the blood. Bit by bit, scarlet feathers emerged, damp and spiky but unmistakable.

Scarcely daring to breathe, Sam concentrated on the torn patch where the feathers joined the skin of his back, then followed the curve of the appendage with his mind. He felt a thrill when it twitched, as naturally as if he'd moved an arm or leg. A little more concentration, and the appendage flared and spread, startling Doctor as it pulled away from his hands.

The tip of the appendage reached out and playfully swiped its soft feathers over Doctor's face, making the scientist laugh.

"Well, Agent Wilson," he asked a pale but triumphant Sam, "how do you like your new wings?"

Chapter 2
Theories of Flight

For two weeks after the procedure, Sam was to be in seclusion, down in the depths of Science Division. Doctor didn't want anyone so much as breathing near the wings until he was sure that they were stable, and Sam's own commander wanted to see what his new secret weapon was capable of before reintroducing him to the unit. Sam was tucked away in a sterile room with a triple-coded lock on the door. So, the very first day after the procedure, it was with some surprise—although not as much as he probably should have felt—that Sam suddenly heard Jon breathe, "Wow," from the supposedly locked doorway.

Sam had been idly flexing the wings, first one, then the other, watching with interest as the feathers rippled when he undulated the muscles. At Jon's voice, he looked up, grinned wildly, and then schooled his expression to something a little less eager. "Did you just hack the locks?"

Jon shrugged in that way that meant "yes". "I think the more important question is, did they give you motherfucking *wings*?"

Sam smiled slyly and mimicked the shrug, making the wing-joints bounce.

Jon returned the smile for a second, but then it faded. "Glad to see that you made it out of Science Division in one piece."

"No extra heads, even!"

"But still…." To Sam's puzzlement, Jon dropped his gaze. He was carrying an armful of books and tablets, and he started drumming those long, clever fingers on the edge of the stack, glancing at the medical instruments beside Sam's bed, at the lights, at the deactivated door alarm that had taken to beeping resentfully at him—everywhere but at Sam. "I'm just saying, you could have told me, man. When I didn't see you in the mess hall yesterday, I—well—and then today, the commander told us you'd be out of commission for a couple of weeks. Didn't say anything more than that. I kinda had to put two and two together and track you down here, make sure you were okay." He finally looked back up at Sam. "You could have mentioned you'd decided to go through with it."

"Sorry." Taken aback at the frank hurt in those grey eyes, Sam blurted out the truth. "I was afraid that if I didn't do it right then, I'd lose my nerve."

Jon looked a little dissatisfied, still, but he nodded. And after a moment, a slow smile spread across his face. "And that would have been a shame; you never would have ended up with *those* beauties."

Sam stretched the wings out further, putting their full span on display. He had to admit, he was getting a thrill out of the hungry way Jon was staring—even if it was at the wings, and not at the rest of him.

With a sudden grin, Jon dashed to his side, hand stretched out towards the red feathers. "Fuck, they're *amazing*. Do they work? What kind of—" He stopped short, his hand an inch from Sam's right wing. "Sorry. May I?"

Sam chuckled. "Go ahead." Jon, with uncharacteristic hesitation, stroked his fingertips over the wing. "And yes, they work; at least a little. I wasn't supposed to test them out yet, but once the science team left me alone yesterday, I gave them a flap and I—" Sam broke off with a choked cry.

Jon glanced up, alarmed. "You okay?"

Sam bit his lip and nodded, not trusting his voice. When Jon's fingers had found the leading edge of his wing, the touch had sent a jolt of arousal through him. Beneath the feathers, the skin there was unbearably sensitive, even to air currents, and the warmth of Jon's hand was sweet torture. It got worse when Jon, clearly worried, turned his hand and rubbed over the edge with his knuckles. Sam squirmed, suddenly and acutely aware of how exposed he was, lying under a thin blanket in only his boxers.

"Um—Jon, man, could you—"

"What is going on in here?" Doctor's usually rich voice cracked peevishly. "I explicitly said no visitors!"

Sam started guiltily. "Oh! Doctor, this is Jon Harris, from my unit. He was just coming to check on me, is all. Jon, this is... Doctor."

"Hi." Jon smiled easily. "Sorry about your locks. I can input some better codes for you, if you like. The wings are awesome, by the way."

Looking torn between preening and exploding, Doctor eventually harrumphed and crossed his arms. "Agent—Harris, was it? I understand your concern, but Agent Wilson really must rest. His enhancements are still delicate, and we cannot risk any damage being done at this stage. Frankly, I'm astonished that your commander would allow you to come down here."

"Oh, he doesn't know." Jon's smile turned a little rakish. "Listen, Doc, I'll get going if you like, but do you think I could leave Sam these?" He nodded to the stack of books, now tucked under one arm for safekeeping.

"Very well."

Jon winked at Sam and dropped the stack on his bedside table. "See you soon, buddy." He leaned over to give Sam a quick pat on the shoulder... and his fingers skated over the achingly sensitive skin near the wing joint, the nerves raw around the edges where human flesh gave way to something entirely other. Sam was grateful that Jon turned away, then, and didn't see him shiver at the contact.

Once the door had closed behind Jon, Doctor came to Sam's bedside and picked up his wrist in a desultory way, noting down his pulse on a clipboard. "Well, then, Agent Wilson. How are you feeling? Any pain, weakness?"

Sam shook his head. "I mean, my back still aches, but not more than we talked about."

"Mmm. And how about your reflexes? Any changes there? Any unexpected... *sensitivity*?" Sam glanced up sharply, and found himself faced with a toothy grin.

Jon may not have seen his reaction, but Doctor certainly had.

Sam's eyes went half-lidded; he decided to play it cool, watching Doctor's smile narrowly. "Yeah, I think my reflexes are a little quicker."

"And?" Doctor was pulling on a pair of rubber gloves. Sam swallowed hard.

"They're pretty sensitive. The wings. I mean, I can feel when the air moves, or when someone's standing close to them, even if they aren't touching me."

"Mmm. Let's try a little experiment, shall we? Sit all the way up, and keep facing front." Doctor walked around behind Sam's bed, removing the pillows and stacking them neatly to the side. "Without looking, tell me where my hand is."

Sam closed his eyes. It was much trickier than he'd imagined. The wings were simply feeling too much, bombarding him with sensory information. And each sensation seemed to trigger an instinct. He could feel them under the surface—his wings twitching, tugging him this way and that, preparing to fly.

He concentrated, and tried to pare away each of the sensations one by one. That, there, was the air coming in from under the door. That cool draught of breath across the tops of his wings was from the other side of the room, from where Doctor had left the door to his office open. And *that*—the tiny island of heat—that was Doctor's hand, held a few inches short of touching him.

"Left wing, in the middle."

"Good." The heat shifted; Sam's feathers rippled, following. "And now?"

"Right wing, lower edge. Towards the tip."

"And now?"

"Right wing again, near my shoulder."

Was it Sam's imagination, or was the heat increasing? "And now?" Doctor asked, a distinct purr in his voice.

"Left—left wing, top of the arch."

He jumped, hissing in a breath, as a set of sure, skilled fingers slid over his wing and buried themselves in the feathers. "And now?"

Sam didn't answer for a moment.

"Where is my hand, Sam?"

"On me."

"And how does it feel?" Doctor dragged his fingertips down with glacial slowness. "Remember, honest feedback is very important to the scientific process."

"Doc, *what are you doing*?" Sam had meant it to be stern, but Doctor's thumb started rubbing circles against his wing, and the words came out in an embarrassing gasp.

"Merely testing the limits of your enhanced senses." Doctor abruptly leaned in, his breath on Sam's ear. "It's a lot more fun than taking the serum in the first place, don't you think? And since you've already gone through the pain…"

That hot breath slithered down the back of Sam's neck, as Doctor crouched behind him, both hands now braced on Sam's wings. The scientist huffed out a gust of air at the base of Sam's wing joint, causing the wing to beat violently.

"… *interesting* — why not enjoy the perks?" Doctor petted the other wing for a moment. "Mmmm. They are magnificent, aren't they? I must admit, since so much of my work is rather… ugly… I do get a thrill out of creating something beautiful, for once. All the more so if the user is enjoying them as well." He straightened, hands still on Sam's wings, but just clasping them reassuringly. "What do you say? Shall we continue the experiment?"

Sam tried to calm his ragged breathing and think. Perversely enough, he found that he did trust Doctor; the man might think of him primarily as a test subject, but it was as a prized test subject to be coddled and protected, not one to be discarded lightly. Comforting, in its own disturbing way. And those hands felt treacherously good on his wings.

"All right," he said, his mouth dry. "We'll continue."

He imagined he could hear the smile in Doctor's voice. "*Good.*" And there was the distinct *snap* of gloves being removed.

The very first touch made Sam writhe. Doctor's fingers, intoxicatingly warm now without the gloves, traced swirling patterns, spiking out his feathers in a way that almost verged on pain. Sam could feel himself getting hard; he groaned, tipping his head back, not even trying to hide his reactions now.

Doctor kept one hand stroking through the feathers, and lifted the other to caress Sam's throat. "You're forgetting something, Sam," he murmured.

"Wha — what?"

"You need to *tell* me how it feels." There was the definite suggestion of a smirk in that voice. "Qualitative data may not be the top priority of most scientists, but I've always found such studies very… *stimulating*."

Sam swallowed, feeling Doctor's fingers trace the motion, down to the hollow at the base of his throat. His wings were quivering madly. "It feels — oh, *fuck* — it feels good, Doc."

"Mmmm." Doctor lowered his head to nuzzle at the crook of Sam's shoulder, while returning both his hands to the wings. "Go on."

"So fucking good…" Sam arched back, panting. Every touch was sending an electric charge down the length of his body, straight to his aching cock; his skin felt like it was on fire. He could feel Doctor's tongue flicker out against the nape of his neck, but it was almost lost in the sheer flood of heat as his wings were fondled. "That — right there. Oh, please, right there…"

"Here?" The scientist's voice was rapidly losing its teasing note, and becoming rougher. "You like it here?"

Sam let out a low moan, his hips bucking. "Yeah, just like that…" His wings were practically wrapped around Doctor now, pressing close. Another swipe of the man's thumbs over his sensitive wing-joint, and Sam keened, squirming into the touch. Doctor made a pleased noise deep in his throat, almost a growl, and started *raking* his fingertips hard through Sam's feathers. "Fuck, Doc, that's too much, I can't take it —"

"*I bet you can,*" Doctor whispered against his neck, and Sam snapped. He spun around, grabbing the scientist by the front of his lab coat and pulling him in for a savage kiss.

Doctor stumbled back a little as Sam released him. For a moment, he stood, eyes wide and shocked, staring at the man on the bed. Sam was suddenly and acutely aware of how he looked: flushed and desperate and clearly turned on, with the sheets tenting over his lap and his wings flared wide. He wasn't the only one, however. Doctor's hair had slipped from its impeccable coif to fall over one eye, and he was breathing almost as hard as Sam.

"What's the matter, Doc?" Sam asked softly. "Isn't that a qualitative response?"

Doctor was silent a moment longer, unconsciously straightening his collar, smoothing back his hair.

Then he dove towards Sam, taking his face in both hands to kiss him. Sam moaned into Doctor's mouth, reaching up to bring his arms around his neck; but Doctor gently pried his hands loose, shushing him. "No, no, not this time. Let me do this."

Fretfully, Sam sat back, and Doctor shot him a quick grin before swinging himself onto the bed, straddling Sam's lap. Sam whined under his breath as Doctor brushed against his erection.

"Please, Doc — I need — "

"So I see." The teasing voice was back. With a smirk, Doctor leaned forward to plunge both hands into Sam's feathers, making him cry out — the front of the wings turned out to be even more sensitive than the back. Without even thinking, Sam was thrusting his hips up, and Doctor was moving with him, rutting against him faster and faster, as his hands found the leading edges of Sam's wings and just *squeezed* —

Sam came hard, eyes closed, his whole body bent backwards like a bow. He could hear Doctor, above him, take a long, shuddering breath, and then he felt him climb shakily off the bed. When Sam opened his eyes, Doctor was standing with his back to him.

"Doc…" Sam wasn't quite sure what to say; luckily, Doctor saved him the trouble.

"A most invigorating experiment, Agent Wilson," he said evenly. Then he glanced back at Sam over his shoulder, and a bit of the familiar purr crept back into his voice. "It seems your new wings have all kinds of side benefits, don't they? We shall have to explore those a little further."

With that, he walked calmly back to his office, and shut the door.

Sam lay awake for a long time, staring at that closed door, torn between trying to figure out the implications of what had just happened and guiltily remembering Jon, crouched beside his bed, running an innocent hand over his trembling wings.

Chapter 3
Testing the Wind

The ground was so far below that it seemed to ripple like water. Sam didn't spend more than a second or two looking down; with the ease of long practice, he picked a spot on the horizon and focused there, instead. How many times had he leapt down from a fire escape or rappelled down an elevator shaft? This was going to be no different.

Except that this time, he was going to *fly*.

Hands secured the harness behind him, tugging to make sure the fit was correct. Doctor had insisted on the safety equipment—Sam was "too valuable an experimental product" to risk—despite the eye-rolling from the commander of Covert Ops, who seemed to be of the opinion that if he'd paid through the nose for a flying operative, then an operative with wings who couldn't figure out how to motherfucking use them was a damned embarrassment who deserved to end up liquefied against a rock face.

The commander rarely said any of these things out loud, but he didn't really have to. After a few years under his command, his soldiers had every facial twitch and raised eyebrow memorised.

Jon circled around to the front, his quick fingers running over Sam's chest, checking fastenings and sliding under straps. "Okay, man?" he murmured, low enough so that the scientist and the commander—who were bent over a clipboard some distance away, sniping at each other—couldn't hear.

"Yup." Sam flashed him a grin that he didn't feel. He'd requested that Jon come along once it had been established that he'd need a spotter. "Hey, not my first time at the rodeo, remember?" Which was true enough; they'd already practiced lifting off from the ground, and short drops off a ladder. "Besides, if the wings suddenly stop working, you've got me, right?"

"Of course I do. But these beauties aren't going to let you down." Jon stroked his fingers over the arc of Sam's wing, tracing a warm path down to the tip of his pinion feather.

It was meant to be comforting, but the touch went through him like an electric shock, making Sam squirm helplessly. He hissed in a breath and looked away. When he glanced back, it was just in time to see Jon's eyes fixed on him. This time, they weren't confused. They were wide and startled.

"Shit, man, did I hurt you?"

It would be a convenient excuse, but Sam couldn't bring himself to say, "Yes." He told himself that it was because it wouldn't be fair to make Jon think he'd caused him pain when he hadn't, and it had nothing to do with wanting to keep Jon's hand on his wing. "No, it's okay. I..."

Sam trailed off, suddenly realising that Jon's hand *hadn't* left his wing. In fact, now that Jon knew it wasn't painful, that hand was actually *moving*—rubbing the tail ends of Sam's feathers between chemical-scarred, but agile, fingertips.

"You sure you're okay, Sam?"

Sam raised his head and looked narrowly at him. Jon was the picture of innocence — expression still unsure, eyes still big and submissive—but there was nothing hesitant about that touch. Nothing submissive, either. Sam bit his lip, trying not to hint at the way the spreading warmth was affecting him.

Abruptly, Jon smiled and pulled away. "They're so interesting—the lightness, the way the layers of feathers operate in different ways. Gonna be amazing to see you test these out."

He gave a last tug at the harness and turned away, and Sam let out a quiet breath. Of course. Jon was curious, because when wasn't he? There was nothing deeper to it.

He rather wished he hadn't thought the word "deep", as he spared another quick glance for the bottom of the canyon. "Ready, Sir? Doctor?"

The commander nodded sharply; Doctor hesitated a moment longer, running an appraising look over Sam. "Very well, Agent Wilson. Proceed."

Ready? Sam mouthed to Jon. Jon shot him a thumbs-up.

And Sam jumped.

Two things happened at once that he was completely unprepared for. The first was the wall-like *slam* of the air against his wings as he caught an updraft. He understood the theory — Doctor had had diagrams, and the commander, tactical maps of air currents — but he hadn't known the impact would be so severe. However, the wings themselves seemed to respond on instinct, flaring out and angling to allow the current to carry him.

It was an exhilarating moment, when the air caught him and held him up — it felt like riding a wave. Which would have been a lot more relaxing, were it not for the second thing.

Sam hadn't anticipated how good — how *distractingly* good — the rushing air would feel on his wings. Underneath him, it was like a cushion, but it trickled over the sensitive backs of the wings in a thousand little rivulets, snaking their way underneath his feathers. It felt like Jon's touch had, back on the cliff, but multiplied by a thousand — cool fingertips raking over every inch of his wingspan. It was torment.

Sam whimpered, suddenly more aroused than he could ever remember being. He tried to keep his wings steady, his body still, but the teasing sensations were too much. His wings fluttered involuntarily, and his body twisted —

— and in a split-second, the movement broke the cushion of air underneath him. Instead of gliding along, he was abruptly flailing, kicking uselessly at the void below.

Sam was falling.

His wings beat frantically, trying to get some traction on the air. For a sickening moment, it seemed to have no effect at all; then Sam grit his teeth and forced the wings down, up, down, in powerful strokes instead of panicked flutters. That slowed his fall, but it wasn't enough. The cliffs were closing in on him, and the air was too still, the wind not reaching down this far. However hard he struggled, it felt like he was swimming up through molasses. The floor of the canyon was swarming towards him…

And then the rope caught and pulled taut, before tugging him backwards, back into the wind.

Thank you, Jon.

The rope slackened again with a slight bounce, like a bungee cord, and Sam felt himself starting to descend, but this time a few beats of his wings were enough to let him hover. Suspended like a kite on a string, he glanced back at the clifftop. Even at this distance, he could make out Jon's mile-wide grin.

Sam grinned back, relief flooding over him. And then, very cautiously, he dipped his wings to one side in a pilot's salute.

"Remarkable. Absolutely remarkable."

Doctor wasn't even bothering to write on his clipboard, for once; it dangled, forgotten, from his hand as he peered at the display on the panel above Sam's head. "You aren't showing nearly the levels of strain I would have expected from the intensive flights you've had over the past few days. If anything, you seem better able to bear the physical exertion now than you were before the serum. Tell me, how do you feel?"

"Fine," Sam answered automatically. At Doctor's slightly impatient look, he elaborated, "Flying doesn't seem to wear me out, however long it lasts. I feel like I'm starving all the time, though—except when I'm actually in the air. I can barely think about food then."

"Yes, your metabolism is shifting, pushing you to shore up calories for longer flights. At this rate, you could probably fly south for the winter if you liked." Doctor's smile was thin, but real; Sam returned it enthusiastically, but he only had Doctor's attention for a brief second, before the scientist was once again absorbed in the readings. "Any other changes? Besides the obvious, of course."

Doctor didn't look at him, but he reached down and idly ran one finger over the arch of Sam's left wing. Sam shivered on cue, hating himself a little for being so easy to predict.

These appointments always ended the same way. Doctor would start teasing Sam's wings, usually in an offhanded fashion; sometimes he'd only do it for a moment or two, while at other times, he'd continue until Sam was bucking and writhing helplessly, on the verge of begging… and then the touches would stop. Doctor hadn't kissed him again, not after that first time. Sam couldn't pretend that he didn't enjoy the skilful touches on his wings — and more than that, the freedom to respond to them. There was something about the scientist's fascination with his reactions that drove any possibility of shame right out of Sam's head. But it was frustrating. Not just the way the caresses always left him hard and gasping and unsatisfied, either. Sam often found himself watching Doctor, wondering what the hell was going through the man's mind during these sessions.

Maybe it was time to find out.

"Hey, Doc."

"Hmm?" With his right hand, Doctor was adjusting the line that ran from one of the sensors on Sam's bare chest to the monitor on the wall. The touch was fussy, clinical; Doctor's fingertips never left the small circle of plastic to so much as brush against Sam's skin. His left hand, however, was combing roughly through Sam's feathers, scratching at the down underneath in *that* way that usually left Sam unable to form words. Today, though, Sam tried to push the sensations out of his mind, and concentrate.

"How long is this going to last?" Both of Doctor's hands stilled at the question. "The sensitivity," Sam clarified.

"Oh. Yes. Well, the wings will always be more sensitive than most of your body, but it won't remain at this pitch forever; you've probably already found that it's fading." Again, the flash of a smile. "Think of it this way: you'd react if someone stuck their hand down your pants, but you don't walk around all day thinking about the sensation of your underwear against your skin."

The scientist's hands started to move again, but Sam reached up and slid his right hand over Doctor's left, nestling both their fingers deeper into his feathers. "And how long is *this* going to last?" he asked softly.

Doctor didn't meet Sam's eyes; he seemed transfixed instead by their joined hands. "I—" He swallowed, hard. "That is, daily medical examinations will be required at least until you resume active duty, and then they should be conducted regularly after that point. Of course, if any part of the exam should become... a burden to you." Those bright blue eyes flickered up slowly, finally coming to rest on Sam's. "The — the testing of your new senses, for example..."

Sam considered for a moment, slowly stroking Doctor's hand as he did so. "No. No, we can continue." He smiled hopefully. "Hey, testing those senses is important, right? Gotta know just… how *hard* this is affecting me."

The innuendo—coupled with a slight wiggle of Sam's wing under Doctor's touch—was broad enough to make the scientist smirk. "Of course." His eyes suddenly lit up. "In fact—purely in the interests of science, of course—I would suggest a more controlled experiment. Let's see *exactly* how sensitive you are."

Sam frowned as Doctor turned away from him, fiddling with the settings on the monitor. "What—"

"Remove your boxers, please." The tone was coolly commanding. Feeling nervous and excited at once, Sam quickly stripped off the last of his clothes, and propped himself up on his elbows, watching Doctor's delicate hands reset a dial. Those long fingers strung an additional wire from the monitor, threading it across to the bed—

—and patting a sensor firmly into place on the side of Sam's half-hard cock.

Sam squirmed, the plastic tickling him. "Is that really necessary?"

"Science!" Doctor reprimanded him, winking cheekily, as he attached a second sensor to the other side. Under the quickening beep of the heart monitor, another pulsing beat started up, not quite in tune with it.

Sam wondered whether he should stop this. And yet—there was something perversely arousing about seeing his dick like that, trussed up between two wires, openly displayed for Doctor's intense scrutiny. His cock jumped slightly at the thought, then Sam moaned aloud as Doctor buried both hands in his feathers.

"Mmm, very interesting. Arousal is extremely rapid upon stimulation." Doctor's voice was still flawlessly smooth and detached, but he was speaking low now, right next to Sam's ear. "Shall we see which part is the most sensitive? Test site A…" His hands curled around the arches of Sam's wings and stroked hard. Sam was fully erect now, precome glistening on the tip of his cock. "Promising. *Very*. And how about test site B?"

Fingertips grazing over the fronts of his wings brought Sam close to purring, arching up into the touch. "Hmmmm." Doctor frowned at the monitor, and reached around to tweak the sensors on Sam's cock. Having that warm hand so close to him was too tempting; Sam wanted to rub up against it, have it wrap around his erection and finally give him the contact he was desperate for. But he imagined that was likely to break the spell. After a moment, Doctor's hand moved away… only to settle on the bottom edge of Sam's wing.

"And test site C," Doctor murmured huskily. Those edges were sensitive, as the feathers there were crucial for balance and navigation; they had to respond instantly to changes in the air. That meant that the skin under the feathers was packed with nerves, and shivered violently at Doctor's expert touch. Sam was writhing now, and the second pulse on the monitor was fluttering as his blood started to pound faster.

And then the sensors themselves suddenly started *buzzing*, sending a powerful vibration through his cock. Sam yelled in shock, just as Doctor breathed, "Test site D," against his neck, and latched both hands onto the vulnerable joints of his wings.

Overwhelmed, Sam bucked his hips and came, watching in a daze as his own come pooled on the bare, trembling skin of his stomach.

"There, now. Wasn't that enlightening?" Doctor rested his hand on the top of Sam's head for a moment, then efficiently detached all the sensors from him and tidied the wires away. Sam could tell that the scientist was hard from watching the display he'd just put on, but neither of them mentioned it. After his first few offers to help Doctor out in turn were cheerfully rebuffed, Sam had stopped asking.

Instead, he lay back down, his wings practically wrung out from the overstimulation. "Yeah," he murmured. "Enlightening."

That night, just as Sam was almost at the point of drifting off (still on his hospital bed in Science Division; Doctor was insisting that Sam stay confined there between test flights until he was fully cleared for active duty again), he heard a voice say, "Pssst."

"You know," Sam muttered sleepily, "I've seen that word written down, but I've never actually heard anyone say it before. I don't think it's actually supposed to be a word—just, like, a hissing sound." He cracked one eye open. "Didn't you *just* help Doctor reprogram the locking codes on that door?"

"Yup. And I kept a copy of them." Jon was waggling a bottle of beer in Sam's face. "Contraband."

"Oh, thank Christ." Sam swung his legs down from the bed and gratefully took the bottle, which Jon had already opened for him. "You know, you'd think it would occur to *someone* in the command structure that if a man's just had his entire body mutated to allow him to fly, that man could really use a drink."

Jon flopped down on the bed beside him, and they drank side by side in silence for a while.

"Hey, d'you finish that book I brought you last time? The military thriller?"

Sam nodded at the bedside table. "I'm about halfway in. I've figured it out, though: the general's son is the traitor."

Jon burst out laughing, then quickly muffled it, reflexively glancing towards Doctor's dark office. "That's just like you. I bet you lost interest as soon as you thought you'd cracked it, didn't you?" Sam pulled a face, and Jon poked him lightly in the chest. "Well, I'm not telling you whether you're right or not yet—"

"Because *you know I am.*"

"—because you're going to have to finish the book to find out. And I bet the rest of it will surprise you."

"I doubt it, honestly. I mean, nothing against the book; it's good, and you brought it to me just as I was finishing the last of that stack you left me with, so it's all that's kept me from going stir-crazy for the past few days, *thank you.* But books like that rarely really surprise you. They mess you around by throwing a lot of unnecessary details in— and *you* fall for that, because you always overthink shit." Sam rested an elbow on Jon's shoulder. "Most things aren't that complicated."

That set Jon off again, and he clapped a hand over his mouth as his shoulders shook with laughter.

"What?"

"Things aren't that complicated!" Jon finally stuttered out, once he'd gotten a bit more control over himself. "I'm sitting here, in a secure science facility I broke into, next to a man with fucking *wings* who's telling me things aren't complicated!"

Sam snorted at that, and Jon collapsed against him, still giggling. "Yeah, but—they aren't," Sam replied softly. "Even the wings. It's just a question of getting used to them."

"And... are you used to them yet?" Jon's head was still lolling against Sam's chest, in the crook of his shoulder; when he tilted his head up to speak, his mouth and Sam's were only a few inches apart. Sam tensed.

"No, not really," he managed. "Not yet."

Truer words were never spoken, he thought ruefully. He was able to keep up his poker face, even when he was whispering so close to Jon's lips; but poker wings were a different story. They'd flared out in excitement when Jon had leaned against him, and now they were trembling minutely. God*damn* the things.

Jon's hand was on his knee. It might have been a romantic gesture, if it weren't the hand holding Jon's beer, which was leaving a damp circle on Sam's pyjama bottoms. But the hand itself was still wonderfully warm. Jon sighed quietly. "Wish they'd let you out of this place."

"What—you miss me or something?" Sam's jovial tone sounded fake even to his ears.

Jon pulled away very slightly to look up at him. In the dim room, he looked like a sketch done in charcoal, all pale skin and the heavy, black curves of his hair and eyelashes. Even his eyes were black in this light. And he was staring—not a hint of a smile on his face, just staring. At Sam's mouth.

And then, just like that, Jon cracked a grin, and the strange moment had passed. "Yeah. I miss having a big motherfucker like you to dive behind when the guns start going off."

Sam laughed, and put an arm around Jon, drawing him in close. "Dive behind Calhoun. He's built like a brick shithouse."

"Yeah, but he's faster than me; he's usually diving behind *me* before I get the chance."

On impulse, Sam stretched his left wing out behind Jon's back, and carefully — very carefully—curled it around him like a loose, feathery shield. Jon glanced up, startled, then smiled.

Then he gave the wing a reassuring pat. And if Sam shivered, he hid it well.

Chapter 4
Perfect Storm

Blam. Blam. Blam. Blam. Blam. Blam.

On the next round, the hammer clicked uselessly against the empty chamber, and Sam spared a moment to frown at the gun. Had that really been an entire clip? Wasn't he normally better at keeping track than that?

He wasn't technically supposed to be on the shooting range—wasn't really supposed to be out of Science Division, except for his supervised test flights (Doctor insisted that bed rest was even more essential, given the strain he was putting on his body). And he definitely wasn't supposed to be prowling areas of the base where other soldiers, who had yet to be informed of the experiment, could see him—the commander of Covert Ops had plans for a grand unveiling at the next command staff briefing, once Sam's powers of flight were reliable enough to show off.

Sam did feel a little guilty. Flouting the rules wasn't like him. But his body felt so different that it was overwhelming, and some part of him needed to see whether he could still count on it to do what he'd been trained for since he left high school.

He punched a button, and the results of his target practice appeared on a screen to his right (no outmoded paper targets for the agency). Sam grimaced. If he'd been hoping that the practice would help ground him, stop him feeling so altered and adrift, then he'd been wrong. Every shot was off—not by much, true, but his ranking was worse than it had been since he was a trainee.

Swearing very quietly to himself, he turned to choose a different weapon from the wall, and whirled back when he heard a shout of laughter from the corridor. A second later, half the soldiers in Sam's unit — Jon among them — were stepping through the door.

And stopping so short that they nearly piled into one another, as they all stared at Sam.

Calhoun whistled low, and then there was a silence. Then Ng said under her breath, *"Goddamn."*

That seemed to open the floodgates, and before Sam knew it, his teammates were surrounding him, all talking at once.

The hell? — So this is what happened to you, man! — Freakiest goddamn shit I ever saw — Do they work? — What did they do to you? — Okay, that's fucking weird — Can you really fly?

Sam felt his bad mood melting away. Sure, the commander might not be too happy that his secret weapon got out of the bag a little early, but Sam hadn't realised exactly how much he'd missed his team until now. Grinning and motioning for them to stand back, he flapped his wings just enough to allow him to hover off the floor.

The other agents' jaws dropped — apart from Jon, who was hanging back, leaning against the door frame and smiling smugly as he watched. Sam gave one last beat and landed, bowing with a flourish.

"Man, that is *sick*," Calhoun said with relish, and reached out to run his hand over the nearest wing.

Sam flinched back. "Hey, careful, okay? They're, uh — they're still a little tender."

"Aw, c'mon." Lewis pouted, crouching in front of Sam and reaching up to examine the tips of his feathers. "You *gotta* let us look. You've been gone for *weeks*, man, and you know what the commander's like — he never tells us anything. We've been dying to see what they did to you."

Her fingers were unfailingly gentle, and the minute exploration of his feathers was almost soothing at first. But with Calhoun stroking both hands in broad sweeps over the other wing, and Ng's curious hands behind him now, getting perilously close to the over-sensitive wing joints, Sam could feel himself starting to heat up again. He knew he must be blushing bright red. "Look, if it's — "

"Leave him alone, guys," Jon said suddenly. "He's serious, you know — Sam here is a valuable agency resource, and if you even loosen a feather, that red-headed freakshow in Science Division will skin you alive. And then he'll probably take your internal organs to build some kind of giant pancreas gun." He was smirking.

"It's just until they really heal up," Sam lied smoothly. Well, there was a chance that it wasn't quite a lie—with any luck, the maddening sensitivity would fade over time as he got used to the wings. At the very least, though, it was an excuse he could hopefully spin out until his teammates eventually lost interest. "But you can *ask* me anything you want about them in the meantime."

"What do they feel like?" Ng jumped in.

"It was a little like wearing a pack at first—a pretty light one—but now I don't even notice the weight. It's like you don't notice the weight of your arms. There's stuff I can't do, though—can't really sleep flat on my back anymore, and it took a while before I stopped tipping over when I stood up." He smiled. "Can't wear normal clothes, either; they made me a few of these uniforms with the holes in the back and the Velcro."

"Did it hurt, getting them?"

The smile faded, just a touch. "Some, yeah."

"How high can you get?" Calhoun wanted to know.

"High enough that I start gasping. They're going to rig me up with an oxygen mask and test my limits a little more. If I don't end up getting sucked into a jet engine, or some shit." Sam laughed. "That'd be a way to go, after all this work, wouldn't it?"

Eventually, the excited questions dwindled, and the team trailed away to pick up their rifles (after first patting Sam on the back—very carefully—and welcoming him back to the land of the living). Sam was relieved that they'd taken it so well, but then, if there was one thing covert agents for shadowy extra-governmental agencies were good at, it was assimilating some pretty weird shit.

Jon followed them, playfully knocking Sam's shoulder with his own as he went, but stopped when he heard Sam murmur, "Doc isn't a freakshow, you know."

"Pfft, yeah, sure. He injected you with something that turned your DNA inside out when he didn't even know for sure it would work, and now he's keeping you holed up in Science Division like a lab rat in a cage. Nothing weird about any of that."

"He's just—concerned."

"About you? Or about his invention?"

It was the same question that had been bothering Sam — not just about Doctor, either — but it still stung, coming from Jon's mouth. "I'm not a fucking *invention*," Sam growled.

"I didn't mean that. I meant…" Jon trailed off, and his eyes narrowed. "You know what? Forget it. I'm not the one you should be saying that to. Try telling *Doc* instead, if you two are so close."

Sam opened his mouth to object to that idea, but whatever he was about to say died on his lips; at Jon's words, Sam's wings had abruptly and angrily flared out with a sound like a window blind snapping up. Jon raised an eyebrow, glancing at the wings. "Huh. Look at that, you're like Pinocchio. I guess I hit a nerve. Well, if you really like being in Doc's cage so much, you two have fun with that."

With that, he drew a gun from the rack and set about loading it, very deliberately not looking at Sam. Riled, Sam picked up a gun of his own and strode off to practice. Jon's voice stuck in his mind, though, nagging at him, and his shots were wilder than before.

Calhoun took a look over Sam's shoulder. "Aw, *man*. What, those pretty wings taking the blood flow away from your brain?"

"My balance is off," Sam gritted out. "I'll adjust."

"You'd better. Can't always have us hanging around to cover you. Right now, it looks like you need a wingman out there…" He trailed off, shooting another look at Sam, and broke into a broad grin. "Wing… man."

Sam rolled his eyes. From his other side, Ng giggled. "You can be my wingman any time!" she shouted.

"That movie is a million years old, kids," Sam told them casually, and turned back to the target. His next shot went astray, too, missing the target completely, and the recoil made his wings spread out defensively to catch him.

"Whoa! Don't fly away on us, now, Wingman!"

Sam closed his eyes for a second. *This is your team. Yeah, they're fuckwits sometimes, but they're your fuckwits. Remember how glad you were to see them? Pull yourself together.*

Out loud, he said, "Yeah, well, the next time we're on leave and we go to a bar, I think I *will* be your wingman, Ng. I think you need one, considering you haven't been laid since last century."

Ng's jaw dropped, but then she sputtered and burst out laughing. "Hey, fuck you, Wilson! I get laid plenty."

"Oh, yeah? When was the last time you had a guy in your bed? And I'm not counting if Calhoun comes to sleep with you 'cause he's afraid of the dark."

They were all laughing now — except Jon, Sam realised. Ng shoved Sam playfully. "Well, when was the last time *you* had a guy in your bed, *Wingman*?"

"More recently than you, I bet," Sam sniped automatically, giving her a cheeky grin. Which was actually true, he realised with a start, and they'd better not go down *that* road. One of the perks of the agency, as opposed to any, well, *legitimate* armed force, was that it was light on the rules and regs when it came to fraternisation. Still, whatever it was that was happening between him and Doctor, it wasn't exactly something he wanted to shout from the rooftops. Especially around Jon.

… if you two are so close…

Luckily, the conversation had moved on to the lawyer Ng had picked up the last time they were all on leave together, and from there to the question of whether it was better to date within the agency or outside it. Sam almost shot a glance at Jon to gauge his reaction, but thought better of it. Instead, he focused his gaze on the target and let the discussion wash over him, the familiar voices soothing him. After another half hour, he managed three shots in a row that were passably on-target, and looked around with a triumphant grin.

And swore silently. *Better add peripheral vision to the things these damned wings mess up.* Without Sam even realising, Jon had already left.

Sam had snuck back to Science Division, but stealth hadn't helped; it had turned out that Doctor had already noticed his unauthorised absence. After enduring a pointedly thorough examination — to make sure the wings hadn't been "damaged" — Sam had begun hesitantly, "So, Doc — it seems like my balance is still off."

"I'm not surprised. It's a common side effect of hearing loss."

Sam had panicked slightly. "I've got hearing loss?"

"Oh, don't you?" Doctor had angrily scrawled a last note on the clipboard and snapped his pen closed. "Then I have to assume that you *heard* me tell you not to leave Science Division!"

"Jesus, Doc, don't scare me like that."

"I should be telling you the same thing!"

They had glared at each other for a long moment, and Sam had given in first. "I'm sorry. I shouldn't have disobeyed your orders, Doctor. But—I need to be back with my team." And he'd explained, as best he could, the problems with his aim, the need to unearth any other potential issues, the desirability of training together as a unit again... all while trying to keep the longing out of his voice, and the fear.

Doctor had looked at him blankly at first. "But we've started practicing marksmanship, in your sessions with the commander and myself."

"Marksmanship while I'm flying. Turns out that it's different on the ground."

"But you won't be on the ground."

"But I need to be able to be. Even specialised soldiers need to be able to handle the basics."

"You're a little more than a specialised soldier," Doctor had told him, idly ruffling the feathers of one wing. Sam had simply looked at him, until Doctor had sighed and conceded, with a slight pout, "I don't know why your commander wouldn't bring this up, if it's such a strategic necessity, but all right. I will speak to him about it."

"Thank you, Doc."

Now, after a drawn-out meeting with Doctor and the commander, Sam was finally keying in the code for the door to his own quarters once again. It had come at a cost: twice-daily check-ups, and the promise not to venture out, except to visit his teammates or train together. But it was well worth it.

Sam stripped off his uniform and collapsed face-first on his bed, the wings draped out across him like a blanket. Tempting to fall asleep right then, but Sam knew he wouldn't be able to manage it. He was still too keyed up. Jon's voice; Doctor's disapproving pout; the readout from the shooting range, with his misses displayed on it in glaring red—all of them flitted through his mind, one after another. Sam turned restlessly onto his back, spreading his wings out and noticing that they almost brushed the walls of his bedroom. That didn't exactly help. He needed to calm down.

Absently, he reached down, trailing his fingers over his bare stomach before cupping his dick through the fabric of his boxers. He found himself smiling slightly. He'd never felt comfortable jerking off while he was staying in Science Division, not really knowing what kind of surveillance he was under, and his sessions with Doctor made for a less than satisfying (if enjoyable) replacement—so much attention paid to his wings, and almost none to the rest of his body. His own touch was reassuringly familiar.

Shucking the boxers, he drew his fingertips lightly down the length of his cock, feeling it twitch under his hand. At the same time, his wings rustled. Sam's eyes flew open, and he stared at the expanse of scarlet feathers. Even now, they still didn't quite seem like a part of *him*—their reactions were so strong, but still unpredictable, and somehow alien.

Huh. Maybe…

Starting to stroke himself slowly with his right hand, he reached over and gently ran his left over his feathers. The wing shivered a little in response. Encouraged, Sam tried again, weaving his fingers through the feathers; it wasn't as shockingly arousing as when someone else touched them, given that he knew the touch was coming, but it still felt good. Ridiculously good, actually…. Remembering something Doctor had discovered, Sam dug his fingernails in very slightly, lightly scratching at the bases of the feathers. The resulting shudder had him moaning and bucking into his hand.

Closing his eyes again, Sam imagined a man crouched on the bed in front of him. Strong arms flexed, and chiselled shoulders dipped as the shadowed figure leaned forward to take Sam in his mouth. Sam settled into a rhythm, rocking his hips as he tried to conjure up what that hot mouth would feel like sliding down his cock, tongue moving skilfully against him. He thought of the man's hand moving up to caress his wings… no, wait, better, a *second* man, kneeling on the bed next to him, running his hands eagerly through his feathers. Sam caught his breath at the sudden, vivid image of the man losing control and desperately rubbing his body against Sam's wings, the feathers sticking to his sweat-drenched stomach and thighs. The wings quivered as his hand got rougher, raking against the delicate skin under the feathers.

"Mmmm, look at that; I guess I hit a nerve. Don't even try to hide it, Sam. Those pretty wings give you away."

The voice was so clear in his imagination that Sam's eyes flew open; of course, the room was empty, and silent apart from his ragged breath. Feeling stupid, he closed his eyes again, and concentrated.

"Eager, aren't we?" Jon's voice continued. In Sam's mind, the man crouched over him shifted, his body becoming taller and leaner, and achingly familiar. Jon looked up at him, smiling slyly. His lips were just barely brushing Sam's cock. "Want me to keep going, Sam? You want me to suck you until you scream? Until you arch up and come in my mouth?" Jon's tongue snaked out, licking a sinuous trail from the base of Sam's cock to the head. "Fuck, you taste so good, Sam." With that, he swallowed Sam's dick, letting out a soft moan that vibrated against Sam's skin and made him tremble.

Sam's hand was slipping faster over his cock, as he imagined thrusting up in to Jon's obscenely pretty mouth. His other hand was sloppy and frantic, clutching at his wing.

Jon was deep-throating him, his tongue flicking back and forth; there was a look of total, almost blissful concentration on Jon's face that Sam had only ever seen when he was defusing a bomb. Desperate fingers were still working his wings; in the back of his mind, Sam was still picturing a second figure, naked and writhing against his feathers. All his focus was on Jon, though, and the daydream of how that wet, slippery mouth would feel around him, until —

"Oh, come now, Agent Harris. Surely you can do better than that," purred a voice next to Sam's ear.

Sam could see him, clear as day: Doctor sprawled out naked across his wing, hands exploring, whole body rolling in the lush blanket of feathers. Dimly, he knew that in real life, that kind of weight on his wings would hurt, maybe even damage them — but in his imagination, there was nothing but warm pressure and the sight of Doctor's graceful, almost feline form moving on top of him. Doctor tilted his hips, and Sam caught sight of his cock, gliding against Sam's feathers, leaving glistening streaks on the crimson. Sam wasn't easy to embarrass, after so many years of barracks and locker rooms;

still, it made him blush to realise how hard he got, imagining being marked like that.

"You want to come down here and see if you can do any better, Doc?" Jon growled.

Sam was panting, working his cock hard; he was close now, as he pictured Doctor rolling up onto his hands and knees and bending low, his sleek copper hair shimmering next to Jon's messy black tangle. Sam's fingers twisted through his sweat-damp feathers, feeling the way his wings twitched and shuddered in rhythm.

Jon and Doctor were crouched on either side of him now, giving Sam a perfect view as they slowly ran their tongues along his erection. Jon glared a challenge at Doctor, before taking the head of Sam's cock into his mouth and sucking fervently; Sam's breath whined in his chest at the image. And Doctor was lapping at the shaft, his tongue lolling out wantonly.

"I believe the subject finds this *more stimulating, Agent Harris – "*

"Come for me, Sam, want you to fill my mouth – "

"You're nearly there, aren't you, Agent Wilson? Yes – yes *– show us how good it feels – "*

"Sam – god, Sam – come for me – "

Sam bit down on a yell as he came all over his hand, his wings flaring out rigidly, before sagging and folding down over him. Feeling boneless and exhausted, Sam patted the wings gently.

As he turned over to sleep, he let himself imagine Jon nuzzled against him... until he remembered that morning. And lay in the dark for a long time, staring at the ceiling.

Chapter 5
Falling

"Hey, Jon! *Jon!*"

Sam would have preferred to make a more casual approach, but casual didn't mix well with welding tools. Anything that could be remotely classified as 'sneaking up on' Jon while he was wielding that blowtorch was not going to end well.

Jon switched the torch off and pushed his goggles up on his forehead, mussing his hair further. "Sam? What's up? Science Division let you out for recess already?"

Sam winced, and tried to hide it. "Nah, man. I convinced them to let me out for good. I'm back!"

"Huh." Jon wasn't quite looking at him. "I was starting to think you preferred it there."

Sam's eyes narrowed. "This shit again? You think I *like* being poked and prodded—" The memory of exactly *how* he had been prodded made him blush abruptly, and shut his mouth with a snap.

Jon seemed to notice it, too. He still wasn't looking at Sam—preferring to focus on the half-finished chunk of metal screwed to his work bench—but his lips pressed into a thin line. "Well, for someone who doesn't like it, you got pretty defensive about 'Doc' keeping you there. I was starting to wonder whether you enjoyed the attention."

Sam gritted his teeth. He'd come with the intention of apologising, but Jon wasn't exactly making it easy. *Why the hell is he…* And then it clicked into place.

"You're jealous. You're actually fucking *jealous*."

Jon visibly flinched. Then, scowling, he tugged down his goggles and bent to assess the seam he'd been welding.

Of course. Jon the genius. Jon, who's always been the special one. "Listen," Sam practically spat, "you think it's a picnic having these things? It took me a day just to learn to *walk* with them. I'm still figuring out how they work, how they even connect to the rest of me. Why they feel—" Again, Sam sensed that that particular thread of conversation could go in a dangerous direction, and clamped down on it. "I can't *fucking shoot* any more, in case you hadn't noticed. I'm not saying I'd trade them, but it hasn't been easy. And if you think it is, you're more than welcome to sign up for the next batch of Doc's serum." Jon had ripped off the goggles this time, and was staring at Sam. "What?"

"You thought… Sam, I'm not jealous of your *wings*. Christ."

"Uh-huh."

"Hey, I was the one who thought it was a shitty idea in the first place!"

"Until you saw how they turned out! Well, I don't give a shit about the attention. I didn't do this to be some special fucking snowflake, I did it to be—" Sam swallowed, hard. "Useful."

And I'm not. Not like this.

Jon stared, his eyes unreadable, and then looked away, blinking rapidly. They stood like that for a moment, Sam absently rubbing the back of his neck, Jon's fingers tracing the seam in front of him. Then Jon piped up, "You still having trouble shooting?"

"Yeah. It's the balance; plus, the recoil fucks me up."

"What if I made you a different kind of gun?"

"How do you mean?" Sam was intrigued. Everyone had been paying so much attention to studying how his wings worked that until now, no one had suggested developing something to help him work *with* them.

"Lighter. Different balance. Help anchor you." Jon had turned away to dig through his toolbox, and was talking in the staccato shorthand that Sam knew meant he was excited about a new idea.

"Really? That would be… I'd really appreciate that, man." Sam grinned hugely, and Jon looked up just in time to catch it.

And return it.

"You're distracted, Agent Wilson," Doctor murmured, sliding one gloved hand over the arch of his wing.

Sam started. His eyes had been closed; he was relishing the touches, but it was increasingly difficult to keep his mind from wandering. His talk with Jon; training; the new gun; Jon's hands, nimble and calloused, running over the metal seam he'd been welding...

... Jon's mouth, in his mind, wrapped hot and wet around his cock, the corners of his lips turned up in a smirk as he slid wantonly up and down...

It was troubling. Doctor had never exactly set any ground rules for these... sessions, and it wasn't as if their relationship, if you could call it that, extended beyond the bleached-white walls of Science Division. But Sam still felt faintly disloyal for allowing himself to fantasise about Jon while he was under Doctor's hands — even if Doctor himself tended to also feature in those fantasies.

"Sorry, Doc."

Sam couldn't quite hide a disappointed whimper as those skilful hands were abruptly withdrawn from his wings. Doctor scoffed under his breath. "It seems that the heightened sensitivity accompanying the transformation has a limited lifespan. Intriguing... but how disappointing." He bent his head, and appeared to be absorbed in making notes on Sam's chart.

The prospect of being abandoned there, painfully hard and unsatisfied, while Doctor finished his paperwork made Sam squirm. "Uh, Doc..." He was aware that he was blushing. "The... sensitivity is still pretty heightened."

"Oh?" Doctor didn't look up.

Sam swallowed hard. "Please, Doc."

"Please *what*?" He still wasn't looking at Sam, but there was a slight smile playing around the edges of Doctor's mouth, and the smooth rumble of his voice held a predatory note.

"Please touch me. Please stroke my wings. I..." It was tough to get the words out, but Sam was already lying half-naked on a medical bed, writhing, in front of a man who'd made him come countless times just by playing with his wings. Dignity was no longer a viable option. "I need it."

"Mmmm." Doctor put the chart down and stalked towards him, lifting one finger to trace an idle figure-eight over Sam's wing. Sam shivered on cue. "It appears that the effects of stimulation, while delayed, have not entirely lost their potency." He leaned in, his breath warm against Sam's neck; when he spoke, it was in a rough whisper, so different from his normal, sensual purr that it made Sam gasp.

"And I love it when you beg me."

Still, when Sam came, it was to the mental image of Doctor and Jon both, kissing each other savagely, messily, as they lay on top of his wings.

The gun, when it was finished (which was in a record three days, even though Jon kept corralling Sam and making him fire it, then running back to his workshop, muttering calculations), was a thing of beauty—a sleek white tube, almost all plastic instead of metal, and so light that Sam could spin it on one finger, despite the fact that it was the length of a proper sniper rifle. The commander of Covert Ops had been so elated after seeing Sam train with it, both on the ground and in the air, that he'd gone ahead and called a briefing to show off Covert Ops' new super-soldier to Command.

Sam had put his foot down when he'd seen the ridiculous spandex outfit the commander had planned for him. Wind chill, chafing, and the commander's apparent taste in comic books had all been discussed, very calmly and politely, but at great length, until the commander had caved. Kitted out in a modified black agency uniform, Sam had then happily swooped around the canyon outside the base for half an hour, shooting down airborne targets and even performing a few loops for the generals' amusement.

And after he'd landed, answered their questions, accepted their frank admiration with good grace, he'd been dismissed—and had been tackled in the hallway by Jon, who, regardless of Sam's greater bulk, had whooped and hoisted him up in his arms, jealousy apparently forgotten. Sam had been elated, and hoped that Jon hadn't noticed the way Sam had flapped his wings, very slightly, to keep himself aloft in Jon's grasp a little longer.

And now, Sam was free. Free to roam wherever he wanted on the base; free to rejoin his team, not just for training, but on actual missions, and finally make use of his wings.

"Hey, Wingman!"

Of course, there were a few things he was having to get used to.

News of Sam's genetic alteration had spread like wildfire, and with it had come a rush of fascination from the regular troops—the ones who normally steered clear of Covert Ops. At first, they'd just stared; then had come the not-as-subtle-as-they-imagined circling, with those who were bold enough actually approaching to ask questions, while others hung back and whispered to each other. And then had come the nicknames.

Wingman wasn't the worst, by any means. Featherhead had been pretty bad, Chickadee-dee-dee even worse; he hadn't *quite* slugged the guy who'd squawked at him, "Polly wanna cracker?" but he'd leaned in and kind of growled under his breath, in a way that suggested that Polly might have a craving for human flesh instead. But ultimately, Wingman was what his comrades had dubbed him, and Wingman was what stuck.

Sam waved cheerily across the commissary in response to the hail (causing the soldier who'd shouted at him to blush and abruptly duck his head in panic), then turned and plunked his tray down at a relatively empty table. As he stretched luxuriously, the wings unfolded to their full, massive length, flexing and shivering.

His feathers prickled slightly at a shift in the air. A second later, Jon ducked around Sam's extended wing and dropped down next to him, throwing a casual arm around his shoulders.

"Hey, Sam. What the hell are you eating?" With his free hand, Jon picked up Sam's fork and poked his Casserole Surprise delicately; it gave a sickening quiver.

"I don't have an answer to that question, and I don't want one." Sam grabbed the fork, wrestling for a moment with Jon, who was playfully refusing to let go. "But if you don't give me my fork back, I'm force-feeding it to you."

"The casserole or the fork?"

"The casserole. The fork is going up your ass."

"Fucker." But Jon grinned, and let go of the fork, tightening his arm around Sam to draw him close for a second.

Sam smiled, but then abruptly caught his breath. Jon's hand was resting close to the right wing-joint on Sam's back, skating over the achingly sensitive skin that peeked through the slit in the modified uniform; his fingertips were lazily flicking against the soft down that covered the joint itself. The heat of Jon's hand was tantalising, and Sam felt his face flush.

Unacceptable, Wilson. You know it's just Jon being Jon, and if these damned wings weren't turning you into a walking hard-on, you wouldn't think twice about it. He shifted slightly, trying to ignore the touch.

"Seriously, though, man, I always thought that the fr—" Jon shot Sam a quick look. "That is, that Science Division was getting rid of all that bio-hazardous stuff by hiding it in the food here. It's just—I think they skipped the hiding part entirely this time…"

Sam meant to hum in agreement, but the palm of Jon's hand settled directly on his wing joint, softly closing around it, and the sound came out as more of a moan.

Jon pulled back slightly to look at him, but he didn't let go. "You okay?" he asked softly.

"Yeah." Sam shrugged exaggeratedly, resettling Jon's hand to a safer spot between his shoulder blades. "These damn things are giving me a backache, that's all."

"See this?" Jon held his free hand in front of Sam's face, rubbing his thumb and forefinger together. "World's smallest violin, you super-powered motherfucker." His other hand rubbed slow, teasing circles over Sam's wing-joint. "Want me to stop?"

Was it his imagination, or did Jon's voice sound huskier than normal? Sam's gaze snapped to Jon's face. Jon wasn't smiling; he was watching Sam intently.

Then he trailed his fingertips up, tracing the arc of Sam's other wing, from the joint all the way to the tip. Sam couldn't hide it this time—he shuddered violently, eyes squeezing shut.

When they opened, Jon had his trademark grin on again. Mortified, Sam shot him a rigid, artificially bright smile.

"You know," Jon continued casually, still stroking through Sam's feathers as if it were the most natural thing in the world, "it sounds like what you need is a decent massage. I could try to pound out those back muscles for you, if you want."

Fuck you, Jon, don't — don't make fun of me like this, not now. Not when you're touching me like…

Feeling stung, Sam found himself replying, "What, candles and scented oil and everything, lover?" in a voice that sounded — even to his ears — less snarky and more out-and-out cruel.

Jon retreated, throwing his hands up. "Yeah, okay, stupid idea. Just thought I'd ask."

There was something in the way he slumped over the table, avoiding Sam's gaze, that made Sam feel a stab of regret. "I'm kidding, man, don't worry about it." Sam tentatively touched his fork to the rapidly cooling lump of casserole in front of him. It squirmed in a way that really should not be possible. "Drawbacks of being a freak of nature, now, I guess. If there's one thing I — "

And the proximity alarm chose that moment to start blaring through the base. Every agent in the commissary jumped to their feet, pulling flak jackets closed and scooping up weapons as they went. Jon and Sam exchanged a single look before they turned and ran, exactly in step, to where the rest of their unit would be waiting.

"We've got incoming assault drones, bearing mark one one three!"

Sam's unit, along with three others — one also Covert Ops, and two batches of ground troops — rose up out of the mountaintop and into utter chaos. Soldiers were running frantically back and forth, shouting to each other, grabbing new arrivals and hustling them off in all directions. A captain shepherded Sam's group off the stainless steel platform, allowing it to sink back down into the underground base. A moment later, the massive trapdoors slid closed over the elevator shaft, camouflaging it as part of the cliff top. Sam flicked on the radio at his collar — but nothing came out, not even static.

That was when it clicked that everyone seemed to be yelling across the cliff top instead of using their radios. Sam looked around, noticing that the huge anti-aircraft installations that ringed the cliff top had been de-cloaked, but they stood unmanned, their targeting screens black.

The commander of Covert Ops was striding across the cliff top, deep in conversation with one of the generals; Sam, Jon, and the others jogged up just in time to hear the commander ask, "How did they get so damned *close*?"

"Some kind of EM pulse; it's fucking with all our equipment." The general shook her head. "If we hadn't had a scouting party out on a practice mission, we wouldn't even know they were coming. I can't scramble the jets, anti-aircraft is down—we need your snipers."

Without even looking—as if he just trusted them to be there—the commander barked, "Ng, Smith, take your units and get in position. Take down the drones on sight. Wilson, get aloft and get us some intel."

"No time!" the general shouted, pointing.

It started as an angry, concentrated hum—and then a cloud of drones swarmed over the horizon, streaking towards the cliff. For such twisted shapes, with so many whirling blades snaking out of their hulls in every direction, they should not have been so *fast*; Sam barely had time to make it to the cliff's edge before the drones were on them.

Unstrapping the rifle Jon had made for him, Sam took a deep breath, and dove. His wings flared out with a noise like the snap of a sail. The drones were focused on the cliff and its defenders, and on the base it concealed; none of them so much as swerved to investigate this new airborne object that didn't fit any known profile of a plane or missile.

Taking advantage of that, Sam flapped his way above the swarm, and targeted the lead drone. The shot sent sparks arcing out from its body; the drone stuttered to a halt in midair, and fell like a stone. Two more shots sent two of its fellows plunging to the bottom of the canyon, where they vanished in distant bursts of flame.

The drones had noticed him now. Four of them turned aside to rocket upwards towards his position. Sam twisted like a fish in water, evading them, taking a potshot where he could. His heart was pounding, but to be in battle again—it was intoxicating.

One of the drones speeding towards him suddenly dropped, black smoke trailing behind it, a casualty of the snipers on the cliff. Tucking his wings, Sam went streaking into the gap it left in the formation. He was between the drones following him and the ones harrying the defenders on the mountain, now. Dodging an energy bolt from one of the drones behind him, he dove towards the backs of the drones attacking the cliff, firing as he went. One of them fell; another lurched drunkenly, barely managing to stay aloft. Just as he reached the front rank of drones, Sam dipped and rolled out of the way; one of the drones behind him, unable to stop in time, crashed headlong into another of the machines, sending them both to the canyon floor.

Between them, Sam and the snipers were making short work of the drones. Sam was hovering, trying to pick out his next target, when he noticed a dark shape, skulking around the edge of the cliff. One of the drones had slipped through their guard, circling the cliff top, and was now sneaking up behind the defenders—

—heading straight for Jon's position.

Sam was too far to make the shot, too far to yell. Jon was drawing a bead on one of the drones in front of him, and hadn't noticed the one that was now looming behind him, poised to shoot.

Without thinking, Sam folded his wings flat back and went hurtling towards the cliff top like a missile. Aiming his rifle would be impossible at this speed, without risking hitting Jon; instead, he brought his knees to his chest—the drone was buzzing as its weapons powered up—and slammed both feet squarely into the centre of its plating.

The drone's engines hiccuped, and it whirled on Sam, blades spinning. Panting, Sam pressed his rifle to its hull, and fired.

As the drone plummeted, Sam caught sight of Jon, his face bone-white as he took in the scene. Sam saluted cheekily, taking to the sky again to survey the battle. The skies seemed clear; he did a quick calculation in his head, adding the drones he'd disabled and the ones he'd seen the snipers taking down. *Twenty-three, and—twenty-four. That's it. That's the full complement.*

He grinned a bit ruefully. *And damn it, I wasted the one opportunity I'll probably ever have to say something like, 'Abracadabra, motherfucker!' as I shoot—*

It was at that moment that Sam realised he'd miscounted.

Something latched onto the edge of his left wing and *ripped*. He screamed, looking up just in time to see the last drone shudder and burst into flame as a shot from the cliff caught its engine; its grappling claws were coated in blood and scarlet feathers.

And Sam and the drone were both plunging to the canyon floor below.

Chapter 6
Flying

"… losing him…"

"… 'nother pint of blood hooked…"

"… damage is…"

"… up from Science Division, maybe he…"

Sam's eyes slit open blearily. He could faintly perceive shapes, silhouetted against a blinding light. The voices slipped over and under one another, a flow of human sound that was strangely comforting, but held no meaning for him.

Something was pressed against his nose and mouth. He inhaled, and slept again.

The next day or so passed in a drugged blur. Sam was dimly aware of people moving around him, touching his wings, talking to each other. Only Jon actually tried to talk to him; Sam stared into those familiar grey eyes, looming huge out of a face he couldn't quite make out, and gurgled urgently, but couldn't make the words come.

The pain, when he first woke far enough to be conscious of it, was searing. Sam had had no idea how intensely his wings could hurt. They increased his pain medication, and it was enough to put him into an uneasy sleep, but the gash left by the drone's claws still ached.

Doctor happened to visit during one of the few times Sam was lucid, although in retrospect, he wished he hadn't been. It was painful to see Doctor's face crumple in horror as he looked at the shredded wing. He came and stood beside Sam's bed, but didn't speak; only put his hand out, briefly, to ghost over the shape of the wound, before pulling it back as if he'd been burned. Sam began hesitantly, "Doc…" but Doctor was already turning away, fumbling a glowing green vial into the hand of one of the nurses with nothing like his normal grace, before he left without a glance back.

While Doctor didn't return, whatever was in the vial—some kind of derivative of the original serum, they told him—worked wonders. The ache in Sam's damaged wing dwindled to a dull throb, and the gash started to heal much faster than expected. Fast enough, in fact, that Sam found himself walking out of the infirmary less than seventy-two hours after the battle.

Only to find that his unit was off base—Covert Ops had been given a long weekend's leave as a reward for their performance during the battle. Apparently, their taking out the drones had discouraged any subsequent attack, and had given the rest of the troops time to get the base's defences back online. The commander of Covert Ops was startled to see Sam out of his hospital bed, but he sprang to his feet gamely, holding out his hand. "Fine job out there, Wilson. Looks like that whole—*splicing*—thing was the right decision. You did us proud."

Those words were running through Sam's mind now, as he stood under the shower in the locker room, staring at a thin trickle of red running down the drain.

You did us proud.

He clutched at the shower wall with one hand, fighting a wave of nausea. In spite of the treatment, he still couldn't fold the damaged wing properly, and it was throwing his balance off again—even here, even now, he still felt like he was falling.

At least the locker room was empty. Another day, it might have pissed him off to have missed a chance to spend time away from the base, but right now, he was exhausted, and just grateful that there was no one there to see.

"Hey, Sam."

Sam froze, then turned his head and waved half-heartedly. Jon was standing in the doorway, looking strangely uneasy.

"The medics said you'd been discharged. How're you holding up?"

The wings shrugged, causing Sam to wince regretfully a second later. "It was pretty nasty, but it's healing up okay. I'm grounded for a few weeks."

"Shit, I'm sorry. You really took the hit for all of us out there."

"What exactly happened, anyway? After that fucking thing got me? All I remember is falling."

"You managed to get to a ledge—I don't know how, you only had the one good wing and you must've been ready to pass out—and by then the electronics were back online, so we could send a chopper down for you." Jon looked down, his voice cracking. "It was—it was a close call, man. Really fucking close."

Sam lowered his eyes, ducking back under the shower as he tried not to think about what could have happened—or about Jon looking so broken. The hot water felt good soaking through his hair, streaming down his sore back and shoulders. It stung a little when it hit the bloodied patches where his feathers had been torn out, above the now all-but-invisible gash, but there was something sharp and cleansing even about that.

"Sam." It was soft, under the dull roar of the water.

"What?"

"You're not a freak."

At that, Sam raised his head to stare. Almost as an afterthought, he reached behind himself to turn off the shower. *"What?"*

"I just—I've been thinking about this while you've been out. What you said, right before the battle. You do know the wings don't make you a freak, right? No one seriously thinks that." Jon suddenly lifted his head, chin jutting out defiantly. "And if anyone did—"

"You'd beat their face in?" Sam grinned—his first real smile since the battle—but it wasn't unkind. He knew Jon was fully capable of doing it, after all.

Jon smiled, as well; a thin, sly smile. "I was going to say, stick a fragmentation grenade under their bunk. I've got to maintain a sense of style, right?"

Sam actually laughed at that, tipping his head back against the cool shower wall. "Well, don't worry. I don't actually think I'm a freak." Then his smile vanished, as he regarded his torn wing ruefully. "But I hate these things sometimes, I'm not gonna lie. They're so fucking…"

He stopped himself from saying "sensitive", suddenly remembering the way the wings had twitched under Jon's barest touch. "So fucking *delicate*. Not to mention, they add, like, thirty square feet of target area. And even now, I don't always know what they can do, or how they're going to react." Jon was watching him intently; Sam broke off with a wry smile. "Guess I'm just not used to feeling this exposed."

"There are worse things in the world than being a little more exposed, Sam," Jon whispered. Sam glanced down at himself, still naked, and laughed uncomfortably.

That got a laugh out of Jon, too, breaking the tension in the room. "Yeah, not exactly what I meant." And then Jon was moving closer, the flat of his hand stroking over Sam's wet feathers. "I meant this."

Sam caught his breath. "Jon, what—"

"I could never tell," Jon murmured. "Whenever I flirted with you—I couldn't tell whether you were responding, or just playing along, thinking it was all a joke. Maybe hoping it was. Fuck, I didn't know. It wasn't until you got these…" His fingers curled, dragging down the length of the wing, and Sam threw his head back and *hissed*. "I saw the way you reacted to me—*yes,* just like that. God, Sam, I just…." The fingers stilled, buried in the scarlet feathers. "I was never jealous of *you*, you know. I was jealous of all the time you were suddenly spending away from me. I was jealous of Doctor."

Sam blushed hot. Jon eyed him sidelong. "Yeah. I thought there was something going on there."

"*Was.* Past tense. You were right about him, by the way. Not that he's a freak—he's not—but he's more into his inventions than the people they're attached to. And I knew that going in." Swallowing hard, he continued, "Knew it wasn't ever going to be serious with him… because he's not you."

Jon's eyes were wide in the dim light. "*Fuck,* Sam…"

Sam drew his thumb across Jon's cheekbone, struck by the look of hunger in that gaze. "The… the way you make me feel… that's nothing new. The wings just make it a lot harder to hide."

For a moment, they stood frozen like that, Sam cupping Jon's face, Jon's fingers entangled in Sam's feathers. Then Jon suddenly broke into his familiar, wicked grin. "So don't hide it. I've had more than enough time to think about this, so I've got a *hell* of a lot of ideas for how to make these pretty wings twitch. What do you say?"

Sam let out a breath he felt like he'd been holding for years. "I say you've got a pretty fucking cocky mouth on you, Jon," he growled playfully, and slid his fingers into Jon's hair, leaning to kiss him. Jon's mouth opened hot and slick against his; Sam gasped, and tightened his grip on the other man's hair. The wet slide of Jon's tongue over his distracted Sam from Jon's hands settling on his hips, pushing him gently backwards, but the feeling of his wings hitting the damp shower wall brought him up short.

"Really?" he asked, breaking off the kiss. "You want to do this here?"

Jon grinned again, his hair even more of a mess from Sam's fingers. "If you're up for that. I know you're still hurting…" His eyes slid over to the bare patches on Sam's left wing, but Sam was already kissing him again, his hands leaving damp stains on Jon's shirt as he tugged him close.

"Hell yes, I'm up for it." *In every sense of the word,* Sam thought wryly, glancing down at himself; he was getting hard just from the taste of Jon's mouth, and those fingers teasing his feathers. Jon's gaze followed his, that cheeky grin widening.

"*That's* what I'm talking about. Everybody's gone on leave; no one's going to interrupt us here. And it'll give me a chance to test out my first idea." He was already barefoot, and he stripped off his shirt casually, tossing it to one side and starting to work on his belt. Sam had seen Jon naked before — hell, he'd seen pretty much everyone in their unit naked, men and women both, whether it was in the showers or in the infirmary with the tattered scraps of their clothes being cut away from their wounds. It barely registered anymore. But he'd never seen Jon like *this*: skin flushed, breath quick and flustered, his eyes wide as they raked over every inch of Sam's body. Jon's arms and neck were smeared with engine oil here and there — a perpetual souvenir of the work he did — and there was the faint, sweet-bitter smell of sweat and singed metal on him. It was Jon's scent, familiar as his voice or his smile, but in that moment, Sam thought that he'd never smelled anything so enticing…

… *wait.*

Everyone's gone on leave… so why hasn't Jon? It's not like him to turn down leave, and it must be boring as fuck hanging out at base alone, especially since he had no idea when I would get out of the infirmary…

… oh. OH.

Sam stepped forward, carefully prying Jon's hands off his belt and undoing it himself. "Let me. Please." Jon looked up, startled, then closed his eyes as Sam pushed his pants and boxers all the way to the floor, stroking his fingertips up Jon's legs as he came back up. Tracing the line of his hip, the sharp crease where it met his thigh, the bare curve of his lean stomach; drawing fingernails slowly, almost worshipfully, up Jon's chest, circling his hardened nipples without touching, and then sweeping around to scrape tantalisingly over his back. Jon was whimpering, deep in his throat, but Sam took his time, relishing the different textures of Jon's skin, from his sunburnt shoulders to the pale, vulnerable skin of his lower abdomen that shivered when Sam dragged his tongue across it.

Waiting all that time, just to see if I was okay. Always there, always looking out for me. Jesus, Jon.

He turned his head and breathed hot on Jon's cock, smiling to himself as it jumped and Jon's breath hitched. Then Sam licked his way from the base to the tip, flicking his tongue around the head before sucking it slowly between his lips.

"*Fuck.* Sam—Christ, that's good. I didn't—I swear, I was planning ways to blow *your* mind first, not—"

Sam grinned evilly, and pulled his mouth off Jon's shaft with a wet pop. "Well, if you'd prefer to do it your way, you can always tell me to stop."

"*Do I look like I want you to stop?*" The expression on Jon's face set Sam off laughing, burying his face gently against Jon's thigh. Then he settled back on his heels and took Jon's cock all the way in.

The strangled cry from Jon, combined with the way he grabbed hold of the tops of Sam's wings and *squeezed*, made Sam harder than he could have imagined. He moaned around Jon's erection, which caused Jon to start shaking, the muscles in his thighs tensing under Sam's fingers as if to prevent himself from thrusting wildly into Sam's mouth. Sam went slowly, relishing the heat of Jon's skin against his tongue, the salty taste of him. As he sucked, he curled his wings around himself and flexed them, ghosting just the tips of his pinion feathers up the backs of Jon's legs. Jon was groaning, hands stroking roughly over Sam's wings, though he steered well clear of the still-tender wound on the left side. The caresses felt almost too good; those nimble fingertips were setting every nerve on fire, and when Jon raked across the wing-joints, spiking up the soft down in every direction, the intensity was so great that it bordered on pain. Sam's breath was stuttering in his chest. At this rate, he wasn't sure he could hold out much longer than Jon.

Sam looked up, meeting those dazed grey eyes, and moaned again, deliberately. And then he watched as Jon came undone. His head tipped back, chest heaving, and he cried out as a hot spurt of come filled Sam's mouth.

Sam stayed on his knees, hands cradling Jon's hips and wings wrapped around them both, until Jon's breathing steadied. "Sam... *fuck*... I had no idea..."

"Speaking of ideas..." Sam playfully ran one hand over Jon's calf. "What was that idea you said you wanted to test out?"

"Hmm? Oh! Hang on!" Jon's pale form vanished into the shadows of the locker room; when he returned, he was brandishing a wrench.

Sam cringed, his wings folding protectively over his crotch by instinct. "Whoa, okay, look—let's talk about this, yeah?"

Jon blinked at him in surprise, then burst out laughing. "No—no, Sam, it's for the shower. A couple of little adjustments." And with that, he slung one arm up over the nearest showerhead, hoisting himself up and dangling like a monkey to get a better look at the fixture. Stretching down to brace one foot on the floor, he went to work. The tip of his tongue was sticking out one side of his mouth, just as it did whenever he had some elaborate cryptogram to crack—or a ticking bomb to defuse.

Sam watched in amazement, an affectionate smile starting to tug at the corners of his mouth. "Jon, are you... are you *hot-wiring* the showerhead?"

"You could call it that. See, I thought this through. When you shower, your wings probably don't feel wet the way your skin does, right?" Sam nodded, surprised. "Figures—natural waterproofing, makes sure you don't get waterlogged if you have to fly in the rain. But we know that they *are* sensitive to changes in temperature, pressure—" Satisfied, he dropped down and walked to the next show-erhead, pausing to blow on Sam's right wing. His breath stirred the down beneath the feathers, and Sam let out a low moan. "Changes in the air. So, all I'm doing is taking what the showers in this dump do naturally — uneven water pressure, uncertain heat—and enhancing it so that it's a feature instead of a bug."

Sam's brow furrowed. He couldn't remember ever having talked about the waterproofing with Jon—couldn't remember having really thought about it himself, actually. Which meant… "You researched me? I mean, the wings? You went and looked up how they work?" Sam suddenly laughed, shaking his head. "What am I saying? Of course you did."

"Well, yeah." Jon glanced down, suddenly shy. "I told you I'd been thinking about it for—*mmmf.*" While he was speaking, Sam had crossed the distance between then, and cut him off by wrapping one hand around the back of Jon's neck and kissing him. When they finally broke apart, Jon's eyes stayed shut for a moment, his lips parted and reddened.

"So what did you have in mind?"

Jon opened his eyes and winked. "Stand right here, and spread your wings as wide as you can." Sam shifted into position, giving the other man a bemused smile.

And Jon flipped on the showers.

Sam bit back a cry. He couldn't help it. The water was wonderful and torturous all at once. Just when he thought that the pressure drilling relentlessly against his wings was too much to take, one of the showerheads let out a clunk and abruptly shifted to a soft drizzle that teased his sore, over-sensitised wing, while the other showerhead continued to lash at him. The effect was dizzying, and Sam almost lost his balance completely when Jon slid both hands around his waist and bent him backwards, sucking hard at the hollow of Sam's throat.

It was better than flying. It was like being caught in a storm at high altitudes, tossed around like a rag doll, the wind and rain whipping across his wings until they ached—but here he was *safe*. No fear; only exhilaration. Jon's hot mouth trailed lazily down Sam's chest, while the water flashed off, on, scalding, freezing, gentle and punishingly hard. By the time Jon's lips wrapped around his cock, Sam was babbling, any self-consciousness gone as his voice was half-lost in the water's roar.

"Right there, *right there*, oh, fuck, your mouth feels so good… *God*, Jon, it's like I'm coming apart. Suck me, please, I can't take it anymore. Please, please — need that mouth on me, you have no — don't stop, just like that, oh Jon, *Jon* — "

It was the only constant — that impossibly hot, supple mouth, sucking steadily at his dick, grounding him in the midst of his flight. Teetering on the edge, Sam opened his eyes and looked down. The water was running in sheets down the skin of his chest, soaking Jon's hair as he knelt as if in rapture, with his wet lashes resting against his cheekbones and his mouth stretched wide around Sam's cock. Jon was already half-hard again, but he seemed to be ignoring it, holding onto Sam's waist instead and rubbing his thumbs soothingly over the drenched skin.

Sam was close, so close, but there was something more that he needed.

"Jon," he begged hoarsely. Jon looked up at him, squinting against the spray. "Please. Touch my wings."

And there it was — under the beat of the water, those sure, clever fingers running over every inch of his wingspan, eagerly mapping out every curve and ridge. Jon's hands explored the lithe muscles of his wings, now so tense that they were trembling. Where Jon's touch parted the outer feathers, little streams of water soaked through to the down underneath, sharp as tiny electric shocks. Sam's wings shook.

And then Jon took a fistful of feathers in each hand and *tugged*, and Sam screamed.

He felt like he was plummeting, the world whiting out around him. The wings snapped fully open. Dimly, he was aware of Jon staring, his gaze heavy-lidded and starving; and then there was nothing, nothing but the sense of falling.

When he came back to himself, Sam was a quivering wreck, leaning on the clammy shower wall for support, and Jon was reaching out to put his arms around him.

"So goddamn beautiful," Jon murmured against Sam's chest. "Jesus, don't ever hate those wings, Sam. Look at what they can do. Look at what *I* can make you do."

Sam kissed him hard, tasting his own come on Jon's tongue. "Asshole. Next time, I swear — give me some lube and a little warning, and you'll see exactly what I can make *you* do, without any damn wings." Jon laughed, and turned in Sam's arms, leaning back against him.

And Sam folded his wings around them both, and it felt... right.

I love you. He didn't say it out loud; not just yet. Instead, he let out a sigh, pressing his lips to Jon's wet hair. "Hey."

"Mmmm?"

"Soon as this wing heals up... do you want to come flying with me?"

If you enjoyed this story, you can sign up for a free membership at
ForbiddenFiction and discuss it with other readers
and the author at the *Wingman* story page
at http://forbiddenfiction.com/library/story/CK1-1.000145.

Valkyrie's Child

Ann Gimpel

Ann Gimpel is a clinical psychologist with a Jungian bent. Avocations include mountaineering, skiing, wilderness photography and, of course, writing. A lifelong aficionado of the unusual, she began writing speculative fiction a few years ago. She also writes paranormal romance and erotic romance. Her short fiction has appeared in a number of webzines, magazines and anthologies. The Transformation Series trilogy, complete with the publication of *Psyche's Promise* is dystopian, contemporary fantasy.

Chapter 1
Cloudberry Driven

Astyr reached upwards, her body stretched flat against the face of a rock-studded dirt cliff. Taking a deep breath she balanced on tiptoe, scrabbling with her fingertips against the steep hillside. *Ach, I need something to pull myself up with.* Casting about for a likely root, but finding nothing, Astyr cursed helplessly as she stared fixedly at the cloudberries dangling from the cliff's top. Frantically, she searched again for a way to shinny up to the luscious, blush-toned fruits. Their rich odor was making her... hunger, for the berries and other unnamed things as well.

That's the problem now, isn't it? I always want what I'm not supposed to have. A multitude of scars on her body bore mute testament to brutal lashings after the Elder's Council — The Thing — had found her guilty on many occasions. *Why can't I be more like everyone else? It would make things so much easier...* She thought sadly about her wings — the Thing had taken them, too.

"What do you think you're doing?" The voice was shocked — and sharp. Astyr shrank back into herself.

"Nothing," she muttered, carefully arranging her features into what she hoped was a studied neutrality as she shifted nervously from foot to foot. With a surreptitious glance upwards at the fruit, Astyr folded what was left of her wings tightly across her back. Their absence made the openings in the back of her robe a travesty. *Worthless things! Why even have them? I can't fly anymore.* Anger kindled at what her life had become.

This accursed place. It draws me like a lodestone. Wish I could break free. Those berries have meant nothing but trouble. Against will and reason, her eyes strayed upwards once again and a yearning so poignant she nearly gasped seared her.

"Remember what happened that time he caught you?" Ragnhild's voice vibrated as barely suppressed fury mingled with what might have been concern. Outspread black wings quivered with outrage. Her aunt fluttered a few inches off the ground staring balefully at the cloudberries. "He and those wolves of his are depraved."

Folding her wings in a rustle of feathers, Ragnhild touched down and held out her arms. After a brief internal struggle, Astyr's need for comfort won out and she burrowed into those familiar arms, much as she'd done years ago when she was still small.

"Come away from this place." Drawing back from her niece, Ragnhild wrinkled her nose, sniffing at the air. "I mislike the smell. It's... evil somehow. You shouldn't even be here and you know it." Reaching out with one knobby, misshapen index finger, she placed it under Astyr's chin, forcing her gaze upwards. "Why aren't you at your loom with the other maidens?"

"Leiki let me go early," Astyr murmured, hoping her aunt wouldn't know she was lying. She couldn't stand being cooped up in an airless cave with the thrum of the warp and weft threads reverberating like an overactive gong in her head. Ever since the warg who lived on top of the wall had cut off her hair, she hadn't been good for much else, though. It wasn't so much what he'd done—after all, her hair would have grown back—but the Elder's Council had decreed she must forfeit her wings. Resentment simmered. It didn't take much to draw it to the surface. It was true she'd left without permission. And gone where permission would never have been granted. Nevertheless, losing her wings seemed unduly harsh.

Her Clan lived by trading goods, finely woven woolens from the sheep they tended. While the men took care of the flocks and hunted, the women were trained to work enormous floor looms from an early age. Those too young for mates—or too old—or who would never be allowed a husband or children spent their days weaving. *And since no man would want me without wings...*

Gloom settled over Astyr like a winding cloth. Her shoulders sagged. Barely twenty, the specter of the next fifty or sixty years stretched out before her, drab and colorless, until she was too old to sit upright for long hours at a loom. After that, she'd be assigned an easier job such as cleaning or carding wool or, perhaps, she'd be sent to tend a shrine to Gunnr, or another of the Valkyries. Each settlement picked which Valkyrie they wanted as a totem. Gunnr was special to her people.

Astyr bit at her lip. She'd never understood the irony of worshipping a Valkyrie. Clan women were rewarded for passivity, not valor. In her secret places, Astyr had always wanted to be like those virgin warriors who rode the skies, deciding who was to live and who— She blew out a weary breath, feeling even worse. No dreams for her. Not anymore.

In spite of all that, Ragnhild was right to pull her away from the borders of Keir's lands. No matter how wrong it felt, Astyr found herself drawn back again and again. It was almost like there was a damn tether attaching her to those succulent berries... and her memories of Keir. Something compelling and magnetic about his wolf-linked energies swirled in her thoughts as the piquant gingery odor of the cloudberries, dangling from their cliff top, faded slowly away.

That's how he caught me, she mused walking next to Ragnhild. The smell of the berries had been her undoing. Astyr reddened at the memory. It had been one of many times she'd feigned a headache to escape from loom duty.

Thoughts focused on what had happened *after* the lie, Astyr remembered the freedom of that perfect, sun-drenched day. Since she'd had the time, she'd flown farther than usual from home. Just when she'd started thinking it was about time to turn around, she'd come upon the strange fruits—red and amber on stubby, deep green bushes—saturating the indolent warmth of mid-afternoon with a rich, sensual bouquet. Curious what one might taste like, she'd floated down to earth, plucked a nearby candidate from its low-hanging bush and bitten into it. Even now, two years later, she could still feel the burst of ecstasy as the juice heated the inside of her tender mouth setting fire to her nerves.

"It's because you ate them once. That's why you end up back here." Ragnhild had drawn her arthritic hands back under the long, daggèd sleeves of her black matron's gown.

"I hate it when you read my mind," Astyr complained, a brand new blush creeping upwards from the cowl of her shapeless, beige robe. *Hope she doesn't find out I told Leiki I was sick.* Loose strands escaping from wheat-colored braids blew around her face, tugged by a gentle breeze. Eyes cast down as became a maiden, she continued walking towards the collection of caves her Clan called home.

Shuffling a bit, Ragnhild hurried to catch up. Astyr knew if it weren't for her, her aunt would take to the air. "You need to talk about it." Her aunt spoke firmly. "Keeping everything locked up inside isn't helping you at all. For Gunnr's sake, it's been two seasons since that degenerate cut off your hair and you're still aching for whatever you found there. Why you don't fear him is beyond me."

"It's not like he hurt me, Auntie." Seeing Ragnhild's face darken, Astyr hurried on. "It was our own Council—"

"Enough!"

Her aunt's tone stilled her tongue. Astyr retreated into her thoughts. *Yes, two seasons since I ate myself sick on those wretched berries.* She'd passed out, no doubt drunk on the strange fare. When she'd wakened the sky had been darkening into night. Keir sat next to her, caressing her head with one large hand. Her hair, her beautiful three foot long braid, lay on the ground next to him. "Your tresses were so lovely," he rumbled in a deep growl of a voice, "I simply had to have them. Do not fear, maiden, I shall care for these wonderful curls as if they were still a part of you. They smell of you—"

Horrified, she'd bolted from the cloudberry bed, head still muzzy, her thoughts a jumble from the fruit-induced trance. It was only part way down the hill towards home, when she'd instinctively spread her wings for balance and taken to the air, that the enormity of what had occurred hit home. Not only had she lied to Leiki, she was late and the maiden's hair she'd grown since childhood was gone. *Bah! I deserve everything that's happened to me since then. I broke Clan rules and I didn't—*

"Astyr." Her aunt's crisp tones shattered what was becoming a descent into self-pity. "I see through Gunnr's eyes you're still filled with longing for that... that unspeakable monster living in the high meadows. It is his fault your wings are gone. The Council acted only to protect you." Brow furrowed, Ragnhild clasped the Valkyrie pendant, sigil of her office, hanging from woven golden vines circling her neck.

At the sound of the Valkyrie's name, Astyr bowed her head and made an obeisance, touching her forehead with two fingers. Turning towards her aunt, with a faraway look in her multi-colored eyes, she mumbled, "You can't understand. It's like they're calling to me all of the time, begging me to come and eat some more." There was a hesitation. "They say they miss me. That I'm the most beautiful maiden in all the world, and..."

"Silence!" Ragnhild hissed, letting go of the pendant for long enough to make the hooked sign against evil. A sharp slap canted Astyr's head to one side. She rubbed at her stinging cheek, avoiding her aunt's penetrating gaze.

"You are bewitched, niece. On the morrow, we shall set off on a journey to one of Gunnr's shrines to pray for your soul to be shriven of this madness." The older woman hesitated. "I am not sure if I should tell you this, but I have feared for you ever since you were born with those odd eyes of yours. And then you brought that wolf puppy home when you were just a girl. Those creatures are touched by darkness. I still remember how you howled when your uncle pulled that devil's spawn away from you. You sounded just like one of *them*."

Eyes filling with tears, Astyr turned away from her aunt. "It was just a baby," she snuffled. "A baby wolf that had no mother. I didn't mean to *keep* it. I was just going to feed it until it could take care of itself."

"Listen to yourself!" Ragnhild was practically screeching as she made the sign against evil once again. "You would have brought the shadows of Niffleheim into our very caves without a thought as to the consequences. It is long past time for us to deliver you to Gunnr's temple. A few years in Her service will set things right."

"What if I don't want to go?" *What am I saying?* An inner part of her was aghast at the question that had just bubbled past her lips. *What's wrong with me? I know what happens to maidens who go against the Valkyries, or their shaneera handmaidens. We're lost to the darkness and everlasting chill of Niffleheim. No promise of life after life for us.*

Ragnhild stopped walking. Her hands, curled into claws from the crippling disease that was devouring her, grabbed at Astyr's shoulders. They pinched where they held the rough homespun of her gown against tender skin. "You have no choice." She spat the words individually, pausing for emphasis between each one. "If you stay here, it is only a matter of time before you climb back up to gorge on that fruit. The second time there will be no return. Keir will have you. He is... not like us."

"Wh-what is he then?" Astyr's tongue stumbled over the words.

"'Tis best if we do not speak of that." Ragnhild clamped her jaws shut, cutting off the possibility of further dialogue, at least about Keir.

Despite Ragnhild's protestations, Astyr still thought it was the Council's fault she was wingless. Keir couldn't have known what they'd do to her. She dropped her eyes. Looking into her aunt's piercing purple gaze was just too upsetting. Ragnhild's white hair was twisted into multiple braids set with tiny jewels as befitted her rank in their Clan. She was their shaneera, or wise woman. Sometimes Astyr thought Ragnhild could see right into her soul and she felt naked and exposed before the older woman.

"Maybe if I did go to Keir," she mumbled under her breath, "this ache that's with me all the time would ease." Absently, she rubbed at her breastbone trying to soothe away the desire gnawing at her insides.

Watch it. If Auntie was looking into my head, she'd deliver me to The Thing for another session with the whip. Astyr rolled her shoulders, trying to ease the tightness in her muscles. Shutting her eyes momentarily, she imagined a future with Keir. Sometimes she could still feel his big hand stroking her head and it made her ache for... for more of those hands. *Stupid! I'm being incredibly stupid! Auntie must be right. She's our shaneera for a reason.*

Yes, but if she really loved me, she would have taken my side against the Council, another inner voice argued. If she had, I might still have my wings...

Thick, white brows drawing together again, Ragnhild threw a worried glance in Astyr's direction. "Come child," she invited, not unkindly. "It may not be the food you desire, but there is sustenance at home."

As the two women walked side by side through open country, Astyr's thoughts ran in so many directions she felt lightheaded. Lush grasslands cushioned her steps or she might have stumbled. Scrub oaks grew thickly. Young boys drove flocks of sheep towards walled enclosures where they spent the night.

Rising out of nowhere, bouncing off the canyon walls, the sound of Keir's wolves surrounded them, intensifying to a crescendo before fading away. The unruliness of the wolves' song called to Astyr, but she took care to cloak her mind. She didn't know if Ragnhild was paying close enough attention to scry her thoughts, but she didn't want to take any chances. *Maybe I could say I want to go to Gunnr's shrine. Then, when we're skirting Keir's lands, I could break and run. By the time they caught me, I'd be with Keir. Surely he wouldn't let them kill me.*

This is folly, the other half of her argued. I have no idea what he'd do. Not really.

Astyr trembled at the rebellion shooting through her. She tried to temper her runaway thoughts, but her wayward soul practically quivered in anticipation. The idea of losing herself in the cloudberry arbor — and maybe with Keir — was so tantalizing it took her breath away.

Pushing the skins covering the entrance to their cave aside, Astyr made the required veneration at the still pool where a statue of Gunnr presided just beyond the cave's entrance. The winged warrior seemed to be smiling down at her as she knelt, mouthing the expected prayers. *How can she smile on me? Could it be she doesn't know my mind?* Dipping two fingers in the water, Astyr touched both of her eyes, then Gunnr's mouth, before rising. At the far end of the pool, Ullr, god of hunting and all things masculine, stood like an unsmiling beacon radiating displeasure.

Slipping off to the left, Astyr entered the women's quarters. The Moon Folk lived separately, except for unions blessed by the shaneera. And even those couples were only allowed access to one another when the shaneera deemed the woman was fertile and coupling would result in a new life to add to the community. Stripping off her outer robe, Astyr hung it on a post. It was warm in the cave because of the ever-present cook fires. Smoke stung her eyes. "Hello, Mother." Astyr bent to kiss her mother's withered pink cheek and stroke a wing feather back into place.

Sigrath's blind eyes turned, seeking what they would never again be able to see. "I thought it was you," she croaked. The fickle disease that had robbed her of her sight was now working on her vocal cords. "Come, help me with these vegetables so I can finish our evening meal. You're home early, Astyr..."

Chapter 2
Keir's Way

Keir was hunting with some of his wolves. But from a distance. His mind link with Bosu, the pack leader, filled his senses with the smells of a frightened buck that was tiring as the wolves chivied him from multiple directions.

Earlier, he'd sensed the woman. She'd been so close, so very close. He'd placed the fruit purposefully, spreading a particularly ripe vine so its bounty would hang over the edge of the cliff separating his lands from those of the Moon Folk.

What am I going to do with her if she comes back? he asked himself. The thought had no sooner formed when Keir threw back his head and laughed, reaching down to stroke the hardness between his legs. He knew *exactly* what he would do if the woman came within his reach again. For the briefest of moments, he wondered what would happen if he approached the Chieftain of the Moon Folk to ask for her outright. Perhaps he could trade skins or meat... or cloudberry saplings.

He was just turning this idea about in his mind—his hand moving more firmly on his shaft—when Bosu fell upon the deer. *Need to finish*— Picturing the girl naked, spread eagled and begging for him brought him over the edge. Heat erupted from him in long, lazy waves. *Yessss...* His cock stayed hard. The girl had that effect on him, making him half-crazy with wanting her.

Keir walked to where he'd placed the maiden's braid. He lifted the silky strands to his nose and inhaled deeply. Even after all this time, her hair had an exotic, spicy scent that made his groin ache with need. He unwound a section of the braided tresses and brushed the hair around the swollen tip of him. Closing his hand round his shaft again, he captured the hair against his skin. The scent of her intensified as he stroked himself. Keir felt his back arch as his hips thrust forward pressing his cock into his hand as if it were her body. When his climax took him, it was more violent this time, bursting forth in hard spurts as he imagined the heat of her surrounding him. Imagined her arcing beneath him, crying out for more...

Panting, Keir turned his attention to great canines severing the buck's carotid artery. Blood, hot and salty, filled his senses. It was well past time to join his pack to feed. Dusky skin and sharp, black eyes reflected back at him from the pond next to his simple hut. Keir bound his long, dark hair with bone pins. Straightening his tall, muscular body, soft deerskin moved against him like a second skin. He strode briskly towards the kill site, drawn by his link with Bosu. Early on, with the first wolf, he'd worried what would happen after the animal died. Would his link with the pack be lost?

Keir's memory of how he'd come to exist still embarrassed him, though, of course, he'd scarcely had any say in the way of his making. Odin, most cherished of Gods, had fallen in love with one of his virgin Valkyries. One night, after a riotous celebration marking the anniversary of forcing the giants back into Jotunheim, Odin, besotted with mead and Gunnr's dark beauty, had bedded her. Keir had been the result.

Raised alongside Thor, Keir had always known Odin's trueborn son would remain in Valhalla, while he would have to leave. Though it had been long years ago, his hands balled into fists at the unfairness of it all and his stomach muscles clenched.

On the occasion of his majority, Odin had taken him aside and given him two wolves, progeny of his own Geri and Freki. It had taken a day and a night before Odin had finished with all his instructions, and yet another day and a night with Frey showing him how to grow both fruits and vegetables and sharing other secrets as well. Frey had loaded him down with seeds so Keir might have all the bounty of Asgard no matter where he should settle.

Keir had hoped to say farewell to Gunnr, but she'd fled after he'd been weaned. "Forgive me, Keir," she'd said, furtively wiping away a tear—the tears Valkyries never shed. "Whenever I look upon you, I am shamed anew. For that I must leave." All the years of his growing up there'd been tales of her armor glinting in the aurora borealis far in the northern skies, but they'd been just that — rumors. He'd never laid eyes on his mother again. Sometimes he wondered if she still lived or if her sorrow had been the death of her.

After years of wandering, he'd settled in the mountainous valleys above the Moon People's lands. After a time, memories of his youth in the halls of Valhalla dimmed and it seemed his current abode was the only place he'd ever been, time without mind, linked to the children's children of Odin's wolves. It had turned out that the death of one of his animals hadn't mattered at all, as the bond soon re-established itself to the new pack leader. And so it had been for him... until the woman came.

He'd caught her sitting in the rich dirt of his fruit arbor, sticky golden juice running down her chin as she devoured one cloudberry after another, popping them into her mouth by the handful. She'd not known he was there, so he had precious minutes to simply take her in, her hair the color of a summer sun and the reckless exuberance of youth stamped on her freckled features. He still didn't fully understand what had driven him, but he knew he had to have something from her. So, he'd waited patiently until she'd fallen asleep curled round a cloudberry bush, added a bit of a spell to the mix, then carefully clipped her braid close to her head.

Mouth curving downwards into a frown, he remembered how bereft he'd felt when she'd bolted, frightened half out of her wits. *Was it her hair? Was it me, so close to her maidenhead?* Keir just didn't know. *I tried to be gentle,* he thought to himself, determined that if she came back, he'd find a way to make her stay.

As he thought of the maid, his manhood started to swell again. Long-ago memories of other women surfaced. Keir grimaced wryly. *Ah yes, the women.* How they'd flocked to him in Valhalla, some even before his member was capable of producing seed. Though he didn't understand quite why, he'd been chaste since leaving his father's halls. Sudden knowledge that the cloudberry maid — as he'd taken to thinking of her — was who he'd been waiting for, was the one he wanted to spend his days with, spread like a living thing through every sinew. *Wife. I shall take her to wife...*

Lost in his thoughts, Keir was startled when he realized he'd reached the buck. Growling, he moved in, knife at the ready, and cut out the animal's heart. Holding the still-warm, dripping organ, Keir bent his head to eat, half in his own body and half in Bosu's. He knew he needed to keep a close eye on the wolf.

Ah, here it comes... Envy and rage pounded into his mind, the wolf furious at having to surrender the choicest part. Looking up, Keir met the wolf's amber eyes, narrowed his own and raised his upper lip in a grimace approximating a snarl. The large black and silver wolf backed off, hackles at their mid-point, and dropped his gaze, yielding.

Having reestablished dominance, Keir walked back towards his hut, still chewing on the deer heart. Once again, his thoughts turned to the woman. He'd done everything he could think of to entice her to return. If only she'd come back, he'd take care of her. *I can't re-attach her hair — besides it must have grown back by now — but I could give her a child.* Smiling inwardly, he decided it seemed like more than a fair trade. Popping another chunk of deer heart into his mouth, he ducked into his hut and began to stroke the braid, chanting low of love and longing as he cast another spell. Maybe, just maybe, this one would lure her back to him.

Astyr lay wrapped in sleeping skins in her corner of the women's quarters. From time to time the low buzz of her aunt's and mother's voices reached her ears in snatches of conversation. Forcing herself to pay attention, she heard, "...know you don't like to hear this, but she's bewitched... likely that warg kept the hair and is doing something to draw her back to him..."

"Yes, but why?" Her mother's voice was clearer now.

"Not sure." Ragnhild's reply was muffled. "We must take her to Gunnr's shrine for the purification ritual. ...should have done it long past, but I kept hoping surprised it's taken this long for that devil spawn of Odin's to cause trouble for us."

Sigrath mumbled something Astyr couldn't quite make out, then her aunt went on, "Yes, I know we've traded with him off and on, and that some of the men have met up with him out hunting, but 'tis been years now I've been worried something like this would..."

So, they're really going to take me to the shrine. Normally a journey of that distance would be undertaken by wing... except she couldn't fly anymore. *Does that mean we're going to walk?* Astyr considered this. Though she'd never been far from the valley of the Moon People, she'd heard others talking about that shrine. It took two days to fly there, so it might take as much as a week on foot, walking up and down through mountainous terrain.

Any possibility of sleep fled abruptly as she mulled over the prospects of such a journey. She knew there was a group of shaneera living at the shrine, protecting and maintaining it. In fact, all shaneera, including her aunt, had spent time at Gunnr's shrine, or one like it dedicated to another of the Valkyries. It was part of the required apprenticeship for the wise-women. Was that what Ragnhild had in mind for her? Since she couldn't fly, she'd lost any prospects of an approved marriage. It meant she couldn't help with the hunt, either. The men folk were wingless, but they always took a woman or two along when they hunted to overfly the area, locate game and flush it out of hiding.

I don't want to be a priestess, a voice within her cried. Wondering what she did want, she was appalled by the answer that kept bobbing up. *Keir. I want Keir...and the fruit and the wolves. Or, maybe I just need to leave here. I can't even pretend to respect The Thing. The Elders know and have it in for me. Besides, I'm not a child anymore. I'm tired of being told what to do. Since I lost my wings nearly everyone treats me as if I were a devil's spawn myself...* Fingering the scars on her belly and breasts, Astyr thought about the countless times the lash had fallen on her soft flesh, and the humiliation of her nakedness before the men of the Council. Some of them clutched at their crotches while she was whipped. And they'd moaned in ecstasy while cutting off her wings. At first she hadn't understood that her pain excited them. Once she'd put two and two together, she'd felt ill. The Clan had lots of prohibitions about men and women together, but the men could do pretty much whatever they wanted during their Council meetings.

She thought of Keir and his hands. Rising out of nowhere, a strange, raw excitement swept through her. The feelings were so intense, she gasped. Her nipples and that special spot between her legs were on fire, aching for his touch. She moved a hand to her breast, cupping its weight. A finger snaked to her nipple, then another. She rolled the hard nubbin between her fingers, enjoying the way it made her belly tense with pleasure. Guilt sparred with desire. Good girls didn't have such feelings. Her aunt and mother had told her that often enough.

Astyr rolled over on her belly, tightening her thighs together. Her sleeping fur grazing her nipples was almost as good as her fingers had been. Pressure on the dark, private place between her legs made her reach for herself. As her fingers connected with delicate flesh, she squirmed. She knew what she was doing was wrong, but she couldn't make herself stop. Astyr had been here before. It was like there was a point of no return where she simply had to have that special feeling. With a mind of their own, her fingers rubbed faster and harder as sensation shot through her. Back arched like a bow, she clamped a hand over her mouth and bit down to muffle the moan rising from the back of her throat. In her mind she saw Keir above her, his long, dark hair falling over her face and shoulders as he plowed her with that thing the men kept from view. The fingers that had been rubbing slipped farther back, shoving into her. *Keir. I want Keir.*

Eyes wide open, she stared into the dark, trying to quiet her breathing. Thank Gunnr no one had caught her or it would have meant another lashing. The sound of soft snores rose and fell around her. Her mother and aunt seemed to have gone to sleep along with the rest. *If you're going to leave, do it now*, that inner voice urged. *Don't make your family go through the sham — not to mention shame — of packing up for a major journey if you're just going to run away less than an hour from home.*

Frightened half to death, Astyr clutched her sleeping furs closer to her naked body. Even in the throes of indecision, her hands groped for the clothing she'd left folded in a neat pile near her head. Pulling the items on as silently as she could, she focused her mind on what to bring with her. She knew the punishment for what she was contemplating: death by stoning. No, if she did this, there'd be no turning back. She froze. *What if I can't survive on my own? What then?*

Astyr lay back down, heart hammering in her chest. Was what she was contemplating such a fool's errand as all that? If Keir chased her away, could she still go to the shrine on her own? *Can I even find it unaided?* Sighing, she closed her eyes, grinding her teeth together as she struggled to come to a decision. In truth, she wasn't certain she even wanted Keir. He'd have to do a whole lot of apologizing to make up for taking her hair. She'd tried to lie her way out of what happened, but the missing hair had been her undoing. No one had believed she'd cut it herself. Astyr snorted inwardly. Men didn't ask forgiveness. It wasn't in their nature.

The scent of cloudberries filled her nostrils. She sucked it in hungrily. Where had it come from? Searching the darkness of the cave with her eyes, she didn't see a thing, yet there was that bewitching odor. Inhaling deeply again, the scent of ginger, tinged with nutmeg and lavender, blossomed in her heart and made her choice for her.

Spreading out her favorite sleeping skin, she laid her few possessions on the soft rabbit fur. There was her boar-bristle hair brush, her willow toothbrush, her sewing awl, her extra gown—made of a lighter weave for the warm season—and her birth ring and necklace. Girls were given the ring and necklace when their first moon blood appeared. The stones in the jewelry were specially picked by the shaneera to compliment a young girl's energies. They became part of a dowry for women lucky enough to be allowed a mate.

Astyr shook her head, knowing she needed to hurry. *I can think about this later.* Moving silently as one of her mother's feral cats, she gathered her things, picked up her reed sandals and tiptoed from the cave she'd been born in. Hesitating at the doorway, she looked back. *Good-bye Mother. Good-bye Aunt Ragnhild.*

Resolve weakened by the anguish sluicing through her, and close-to-immobilized by the enormity of what she was about to do, Astyr knelt before Gunnr's shrine. Bowing her head, she prayed to the Valkyrie, asking her blessing though she had no right to expect it. Touching her lips to the statue, she emerged from the cave into a clear night with stars scattered like a million points of light in the sky above her.

Shoving her bare feet quickly into her sandals, she turned one full circle as she prepared to leave. She knew if she hesitated too long she'd take the craven's way, creeping right back into the cave to await her fate on the morrow.

"Where are you going, girl?" a drowsy voice demanded from behind her.

The sentry! How could I have forgotten? "Just to make water." She tried to sound as sleepy as he. Spinning on her heel, she placed her body so he'd have a difficult time noticing her bundle in the semi-gloom.

"Be quick about it then." The voice sounded a bit more awake.

What should I do? Will he wait to see if I slip back in? Or will he just fall back asleep and forget about me? Trying to make at least one part of what she'd told him true, Astyr walked toward the shallow declination where the Clan left their waste. As she squatted, listening to the sound of her urine splattering on the mound of feces, she felt braver. Moving a short distance away from the smells of the privy, Astyr waited. *If he calls out or comes for me, I can just say I felt dizzy...* But he didn't do anything and, after a while, she gathered her things and walked away from her childhood home.

No one else stopped her. Soon she was climbing the track next to the cliff where the cloudberries had tantalized her earlier that day. A fine sheen of sweat beaded on her fair skin, making her freckles glow in the starlight. The night was cool, but the climb up the steep hill, dragging her bundle with her, made her everyday robe far too warm.

Astyr paused at the crest. She looked about her, catching her breath. The track to the shrine wound off to her right. *I should go that way,* she thought. *A good maiden would go that way... This fantasy with Keir is madness. He's a brute. An animal just like his wolves. I'll find the shrine, study hard and become a shaneera like Auntie. Surely, she'll forgive me when she finds out what I've done.*

Another more insidious thought pushed its way in. *I could go and gather a few handfuls of cloudberries — for my journey. After all, I didn't bring any food. Keir's likely asleep. Even if he's not, he won't be tending the fruit in the middle of the night. He'll never even know I've been there.*

Immensely pleased with her compromise of having a few berries and making the proper choice about traveling to the shrine to devote her life to Gunnr, Astyr walked briskly towards the cloudberry bushes. In just a moment or two their smell hit her full on and, dropping her sleeping fur, she sprinted towards the irresistible odor. Voraciously tearing half a dozen berries off the nearest plant, she sank to the ground, ecstatic as the incredible taste burst on her tongue. *Just like the first time,* she thought. *Just like the first time. No,* better *than the first time.*

Juice flowed down her chin, soaking the collar of her gown. Oblivious of turning into a sticky mess, she pulled another handful of fruit off the vine. Time stopped as she gorged herself on the rose and amber colored berries that suddenly made up her entire universe.

You should leave, her inner voice urged after she'd eaten dozens of berries, but Astyr ignored it, lost in the mystery of the fruit of the Gods of Valhalla. From time to time, her hand strayed between her legs. It was wonderful to be free to touch herself and the berry juice intensified her pleasure. She smeared it on her nipples, reveling in how the delicate points came alive between her fingers. She smeared it between her legs. It made her so much more sensitive, she practically howled with delight. Since it seemed she had all the time in the world, she experimented: light touches, quick touches, long, slow stroking. As the night wore its way towards dawn, Astyr smiled lazily into the darkness, stuffing herself with berries and indulging her lust.

Chapter 3
Retribution

Keir came upon her when the eastern sky was reddening, kissing the tips of the nearby mountaintops with morning fire. Her eyes grew huge when she saw him looking down at her. She pulled her errant hands into her lap.

"It is twice now you have eaten of my fruit." He spoke sternly, his face an unreadable mask. "Because of that, I could make you stay with me."

She wondered if he'd seen her touching herself under her robe. The thought excited her all over again and she pressed her legs together. *What am I doing?* Astyr shook her head hard to clear her thoughts as she scrambled to her feet. Squaring her shoulders, she faced him. "You took my hair when last I was here. Why did you do that?"

His eyebrows drew together, making him look even more formidable. Astyr readied herself to run. Her heart hammered against her ribs. It was hard to swallow. He took a step towards her. "No." She held up both hands. "No closer."

What she needed was an answer to her question. She didn't dare ask a second time. She would have been whipped for asking a man such a thing even once back in her village.

He nodded, fine dark eyes settling on hers. "I am sorry, maiden. I did not mean to cause you grief. But you were just so lovely, lying here in this fruit arbor. I still do not understand what possessed me, but I had to have something of yours to keep. Wait—" a horrified note entered his voice as he stepped around behind her. "What happened to your beautiful wings?" He moved in front of her once again, leaning forward as if her reply was the most important thing in the world.

"The Council took them after you cut off my hair." She held his eyes with hers. Now was not a time to be deferential. Keir needed to see what he was responsible for. Astyr looked deep into him, seeking truth. How did he feel about the pain she'd suffered because of him? The strong bones in his face settled into an expression radiating concern—and sorrow. No one had ever looked at her with such caring, not even her aunt or her mother. But she still needed assurance. "Will you promise to never take anything from me again without my permission? You see what taking my hair cost me."

"By Odin's bones," he pounded a closed fist into an open palm, "this is monstrous. Of course I will ask before taking, but, maiden, that is the least of your problems." Anger radiated from him in waves. The fist pounded his palm again and again. "Just tell me who did this to you. I shall make them pay. You should have come to me long since to avenge you." His hand reached over her shoulder to caress what was left of her wings, poking through the back of her robe.

"I-I did not realize," she stammered, feeling stunned. Astyr's soul took flight. No man had ever sought to protect her before. Nor woman, either. She thought again of Ragnhild standing guard outside the Council chamber while the men severed her wings.

"Tell me who did this monstrous thing. I shall take my wolves and make short work of them."

That he was willing was, perhaps, more important than him starting a blood feud with her people. "No." She shook her head. "I do not want you to do that."

The stern planes of his face softened. "Wherever did a maid learn temperance? I would have thought you would welcome revenge."

She felt color rising in her face. He was challenging her decision—just like any man would. She settled her hands on her hips and stood straighter. "Gunnr is our totem Valkyrie. She—" Astyr's voice ran down. The expression on Keir's face had changed so abruptly it was unsettling. He looked both broken and hopeful at the same time. "What?"

He dropped his face into his hands, inhaling sharply. Apparently he was going to accept her wishes and not race down the hill to slaughter her people. Astyr wanted to go to him, to comfort him since something about Gunnr had upset him, but she held herself back. After a long while, he met her gaze again. "Gunnr was my mother. If your Clan picked her, it must mean she has been here from time to time." He sucked in a ragged breath. "I thought she abandoned me as a child. But she's been here all along..."

Astyr felt glad for him. After all, it was good to know your mother cared about you. That didn't address what was unfinished between them, though. "You're going to respect my wishes—about not killing the Council members?" It seemed he would, but she had to know.

"You have my word. Again, maiden, I am sorry about your hair. And even sorrier about your wings." He bowed deeply from the waist. "Most humbly sorry. I am in your debt. The news you brought me of my mother is wonderful and most unexpected." He grinned at her, the smile making tiny creases around his eyes. Suddenly he didn't look as frightening anymore.

Beginning to believe him, and feeling daring, Astyr sidled to a cloudberry bush. Her hand closed about another berry and she yanked it from its stalk.

"Don't you think you've had enough for one night?" Booming laughter burst out of him, filling the vale as he gazed at his decimated arbor. "If you eat them all, there won't be seeds for us to grow more."

She pulled her hand back then, tilted her head to one side and walked over to Keir. "You never asked me last time, but my name is Astyr."

"And I am Keir."

"Yes, I know that."

"Do you come to me of your own free will, or did your Clan disown you?" Keir looked keenly at her, as if her answer to this question was the crux of something, except she didn't understand quite what it might be. He had the most beautiful eyes, wild and dark as deepest night.

"Of my own free will," she murmured, suddenly shy and overcome with the magnitude of what she had done. Once again, fear gripped her. *What if he doesn't want me? Especially after I almost forced him to apologize to me.*

Smiling, he extended a hand and the fluttering in her belly eased.

"You have told me true, for I have ways of knowing these things. Come, we shall break our fast."

Astyr took his hand a bit awkwardly. "I brought a few things…" she said gesturing over one shoulder. Her face flooded with embarrassment. Would he think her terribly presumptuous? She flinched, stealing a glance at him from beneath lowered lids.

But all he said was, "Show me."

She walked slowly to where she'd dropped the meager bundle of her possessions. Stooping, Keir picked it up and tucked it under one arm, while he draped the other around her shoulders. Guiding her with gentle pressure, he showed her the way to his hut. As soon as they were within the clearing, Bosu padded over to greet them both, licking at Astyr's hand. Fixing her with his liquid, golden stare, he whined a soft greeting, tail thumping softly.

Squatting in front of the wolf, Astyr stroked his rough outer coat as she looked into his eyes. The right one had the slightest cast to it and a black star to one edge of the pupil. "This is the wolf puppy I tried to save," she gasped. "There cannot be two with such eyes." Fingers buried in Bosu's thick coat, she pulled him to her. "Thank Gunnr you found a way to live," she murmured.

"Now I have another reason to make you mine." Keir drew her to her feet once more. "Come within, Astyr. I have waited long for you to seek me out. 'Tis why I asked if you had come of your own free will."

Emboldened — this time it was she who put an arm around him — Astyr walked by his side as she entered her new home. Looking curiously around at the interior of the small dwelling, she spied her hair lovingly mounted on the far wall. Drawn to it, she came closer, stroking its silky fineness with a tentative finger. "If it was me you wanted," she said, "you could have but asked. Then you would have had me whole, not mutilated."

"Your people never would have agreed. They see me as an abomination." He held out a hand to her. "I am sorry. I was just so blinded by wanting you, I did not think — Even if I had, it never would have occurred to me that your own people would do such a hideous thing to one of their own."

She knew he was right. The men probably would have stoned

him if he'd set foot in their village. But she was incredulous he'd validated her feelings about what The Thing had done to her.

Astyr turned to him, a broad smile on her face, eyes alight with joy. For the first time since she'd lost her wings, she felt like her life wasn't over after all. "Don't you see? None of that matters now that I'm here with you. You will be my mate..."

As soon as the words left the safety of her throat, color rose, staining her cheeks with embarrassment. She dropped her eyes. *What would Auntie say? Or Mother? A maiden should never be so forward.* "Sorry," she managed to mumble. *Will he punish me now?* She glanced nervously about looking for a cat-o-nine-tails, like the one The Thing used for whippings.

"Sorry for what?" It was Keir's turn to grin. "The women in Valhalla took what they wanted. Maiden, if I am what you want, then I am yours." Closing the distance between them in one long step, he gathered her into his arms. She closed her eyes, turning her face up for the kiss she imagined would happen next. His musky scent was exhilarating. It reminded her of the cloudberries and ever so much more.

When his lips didn't come down on hers, she opened her eyes and pulled back enough to look at him. "D-don't you want t-to kiss me?" She was so embarrassed at having to ask, she could barely get the words out.

"Aye, kissing and... other things," he murmured, running his hands down her back, then lower to cup the curve of her ass. "Right now, I'm enjoying just looking at you and holding you in my arms. It's something I've wanted for a very long time." He pulled her hips close and she felt his manhood jutting against her stomach. Curiosity got the better of embarrassment and she pushed one of her hands between them so she could feel the mysterious thing the men played with under their clothing.

A low moan escaped him. He shoved his hips towards her body to capture her hand as it curled tentatively around his cock. Astyr understood and tightened her grip. Heat flared in her loins a million times hotter than she'd imagined it could.

Keeping a firm grip on her butt with one hand, he tipped her chin up with the other, settling his mouth on hers. His breath tasted like new-mown hay, fresh and clean. When his tongue explored the inside of her mouth, she felt her body melting against him. His member jumped in her hand, startling her. Breaking away from the kiss, she laughed. "Is it alive?"

"Oh, very much so." He laughed, too. "And with a definite mind of its own."

He trailed kisses down the side of her neck, then raised his head to nibble on an earlobe and blow into one of her ears. Her nipples were so taut they ached. Wetness slicked her thighs and she squirmed, pushing her hips against him.

"Here." Moving back from her, he took one of her hands. "I had thought we might share a meal, but that can come later. Come lay with me, maiden." His breath came fast. His skin had taken on a rosy glow. He started leading her towards the corner where the bed was, right underneath her hair.

Can I do this? Stories of maidens who had given their virtue away—and what happened to them afterwards—crowded into her mind. Suddenly Astyr was afraid. Clinging to his hand, she stopped dead. "I-I'm not sure—" she began.

He let go of her hand and looked at her gently. "You are a maid. It is understandable you would be frightened. Just lie down. I have already promised I will not do anything you don't want me to. Besides," he added pragmatically, "you can hardly go back. Your kinsmen will assume you are maid no longer regardless of what happens in this hut. The elders will examine you. They'll get carried away and, if I don't take your maidenhead, they will."

"How do you know?"

"Because I have lived a very long time and I understand men—and women." His hand strayed to the laces keeping his leather breeches in place. In a single, practiced motion, he untied them and let them puddle about his ankles.

He must have stepped out of his breeks, but she didn't notice. All her attention was focused on his cock. It was enormous, and the most beautiful thing she'd ever seen. The wetness on her thighs turned to a flood. One of her hands reached for the secret place between her legs. It needed rubbing in the worst way.

"Uh-uh." He grabbed her hand. "Let me." Moving to her side, he untied the cord at the top of her robe, then pulled the garment over her head, taking care with her wing stubs. His mouth settled on one of her breasts. He suckled a nipple making the most incredible sensations shoot through her nether regions. Well past sentient thought, she pulled his head closer, grinding her nipple against his teeth.

Something touched the inflamed nubbin between her legs. Realizing it was his hand, she pushed into it. He'd only stroked her a few times when her hips developed a mind of their own, bucking against his hand. Gasping, she stifled a moan. No one would hear her all the way up here. Not Auntie, not Mother. But what would Keir think? She was acting like a whore.

"Sorry," she murmured, trying to get her breathing under control. She was aware of her fluids dripping onto the floor. "I'll clean that up."

He laughed. "Bosu will lick it up when he comes inside. Is my bed looking any better?"

Heat rose to her face. She couldn't look at him, but she nodded. He took her hand and guided it to his cock. "There's more," he said. "Lots more. Come on."

He laid her on the bed, hands moving up and down her body. His mouth captured a nipple again, then moved lower. When the heat from his mouth settled over her cunt, she cried out. She'd never felt anything so intense. His tongue flicked out, teasing her sensitive tissue. Groaning, she reached down, twining fingers in his dark hair. He licked and kissed until she was almost to that place where the wonder would start again. Her hips moved rhythmically against his tongue. Her breath came in little, panting gasps.

He slithered up her body. "I think you're ready," he said, voice raspy with passion. "I'll try to be gentle." Pushing her legs wide, he guided himself into her. He went slowly, ever so slowly. Astyr felt her body stretching as he entered her. Once fully inside, he lay quietly, letting her get used to the feel of his cock. She wriggled. It brought the place she always touched in contact with the base of his member. It felt incredibly good. Pushing upwards, she wriggled some more.

The sensation was different, but she was sure she could get to that special place where everything melted if she just kept on rubbing herself against him. Then he started to move. Long, slow strokes heated her flesh. Her nipples pebbled into hard points of delight where they rubbed against his body. She moved faster, wrapping her legs around him. It wouldn't take much more, she thought. Not much more at all. And then it was happening. Sensation swirled through her. It was so intense, she almost couldn't stand it.

He jammed his hands underneath her buttocks and pulled her to him hard. His strokes came faster; his breath was hot against her neck. She felt his cock dancing inside her as it released. Keir moaned, crying her name again and again. He pushed a hand between them and rubbed her magic place fast and hard. Before Astyr knew what was happening, she came again, hips bucking against his hand.

He cradled her against him, murmuring to her in a language she didn't know. Sated, eyes heavy, Astyr felt happy for the first time in years. "Sleep, little one," he said. "There will be time for everything now we've found each other."

Bosu's barking woke her. Astyr rolled over, stretching luxuriantly. Then she remembered. Her hand strayed between her legs. No, she hadn't dreamed it. Her thighs were coated with dried fluids. She heard Keir's voice. Then Auntie's.

Auntie. Oh no! Astyr leapt from the bed, plucked her robe from the floor and settled it over her head. She let herself out the cabin door in time to hear Keir say, "She is wife to me. You no longer have jurisdiction over her."

"Wife? Who performed the ceremony?" Auntie sounded as haughty as ever.

"It was blessed by Odin," Keir informed her. "I am one of his sons."

Astyr stepped to his side, snaking an arm around his waist. "Hello, Auntie."

Ragnhild didn't pay any attention to her. "Odin's son or no. I am here to take my niece back."

"I do not think so," Keir said agreeably enough, though his tone was cold. "I was raised in Valhalla. I can call the wrath of the gods down on you, woman. You must treat my wife with the respect she deserves. She is no longer a child for you to order about."

Astyr moved towards Ragnhild, laying a hand on the older woman's arm. "Auntie, please don't worry about me. Don't you see, I never could have had any sort of life with the Clan. Not after the Council took my wings."

"That is why you were to go to Gunnr's shrine," her aunt said stiffly.

"Yes, and I would have gone if Keir did not want me."

"How can you—?" Red splotches splayed across Ragnhild's cheeks.

Keir stepped between the two women. "You will leave now," he ground out through clenched teeth. "I would have gone to your village and destroyed those who took Astyr's wings, but she held me back."

Ragnhild's eyes sought Keir's. "You would have done what?" she asked incredulously.

"You heard me, woman." He looked at her appraisingly. "You are the shaneera. I can tell by your garb. Your job is to protect the women in your Clan." His lips drew back from his teeth in a snarl that would have done Bosu proud. "You failed. You let your ignorant, arrogant men folk take Astyr's beautiful wings. Be gone before I do something I regret."

"I must think on this. And pray to Gunnr for guidance." Ragnhild sounded rattled.

"No, what you must do is leave. Gunnr is my mother. She would be shamed hearing her name fall from your lips."

Ragnhild turned to go. When she was a few paces away from the hut's open door, she spread her wings, letting the air currents carry her to the Moon People's village below.

Keir came up behind Astyr and put his arms around her. Bosu licked her hand. "Are you sad, my love? I know she was kin to you."

Astyr turned in his arms, laying her head against his chest. "The sad part is she didn't save me from the Elder's Council all those times she could have. My life with the Clan ended two years ago." She pulled back to smile at him. "My new life is here—with you. I'm glad I finally followed my heart."

"So am I." He bent to kiss her. "Too bad it took you so long. Think how much fun we could have had." He settled a hand over her rump and gave it a squeeze.

"It will take time for me to feel really and truly safe," she said in a burst of honesty.

"Of course it will," he murmured against her hair. "Tell me what you need, Astyr. I want to make you happy."

When he said that, she realized she was happy. So much so, she was afraid she'd burst with the feelings. Her stomach rumbled, bringing her back to more practical matters. "You said something about eating a while ago. What can I cook us for breakfast?"

If you enjoyed this story, you can sign up for a free membership at
ForbiddenFiction and discuss it with other readers
and the author at the *Valkyrie's Child* story page
at http://forbiddenfiction.com/library/story/AG1-1.000078.

Underneath It All

Kailin Morgan

Kailin Morgan has always been an avid reader. She discovered goth and industrial music and vampires and werewolves at about the same time. She rediscovered the love of writing through fan-fiction and has since quickly become addicted to the thrill of discovering new characters. Although most of her writing is m/m, she also loves writing strong female characters. Her writing tends towards fantasy, dealing with gods and monsters, but she loves to place them into everyday settings and see what happens.

Chapter 1
Sounds in the Dark

Amy shivered as she hurried along the street. Winter was drawing in and the air was chill with mist and the soft drizzle of the rain which hadn't stopped in days. She glanced up from under the hood of her coat, spotting the grimy white and red of the tube sign.

She looked both ways out of habit, but traffic was strangely light and she took advantage, dashing quickly across the road. Her Converses were letting in water and she squeaked and squelched as she stepped on to the tiled floor of the station.

As usual, the ticket stations were unmanned, the machines blinking their glowing lights silently at her. She wiped her damp fingers vainly against the edge of her t-shirt before scrabbling in her handbag for the travel pass. Amy clutched her bag tighter as she rifled through the contents, fingers failing to connect with the smooth plastic of her pass holder.

"Dammit, no way." Tears threatened at the thought of having lost her pass. There was no way she could afford to replace it. A chill wind blew in through the open doorway, sending goosebumps chasing up and down the nape of her neck. Amy shivered again, curling in on herself, huddling deeper into her coat. A brief image flashed through her mind, the tube station earlier when she had been on her way to work. It had been so busy and then the pregnant woman in front of her had gone down, fainted. Amy had shoved her travel ticket into her pocket, rushing forward to help.

Cold fingers went to her pocket, a sigh of relief gusting out of her as she felt the cool ridge of the plastic holder. Amy zipped her bag closed again, tucking it closely against her body, before she pulled her pass out, hurrying over to the automatic barriers. She swiped her card against the sensor, watching for the little green tick that told her she could enter the station.

She glanced around again as she passed through. The station was deserted, her footsteps echoing off the tile as she made her way over to the escalator. A hand drawn sign informed her that the escalator was out of order and to please use the stairs. A scrawled arrow below pointed over to her right.

Amy sighed again. *At least this would count as a workout, right?* Maybe she would stop off at the corner shop and treat herself to some chocolate, maybe some wine. A pained laugh snorted out of her. Who was she kidding? She had barely managed to make her rent this month, despite living way out in the back of beyond. She hurried over to the stairs. If she didn't make this train, she would have to take the last one; which meant getting off in the centre of the city and swapping lines followed by a long walk in the cold, wet dark.

She pushed open the door to the stairwell, glancing up at the security camera in the corner. The light at the top of the stairs flickered fitfully, casting eerie shadows down the silent steps. Amy wrapped her arms around herself briefly, feeling an ominous shudder track down her spine. She felt the sudden urge to dash out of the station, back out to stand under the wide open sky. She swallowed it down and began her descent.

The steps switch-backed several times as Amy headed down, her thighs and ankles protesting at the speed she took them. The walls seemed to tighten around her, the stairwell closing in on her. Amy sucked in a breath, the sound harsh in the silence. Walls didn't move. It was simply a matter of anxiety causing hormones and other chemicals to flood her bloodstream, making her heart speed up and her muscles flush with blood in case she had to evade an enemy.

Amy ran through the names of hormones and the glands that secreted them, concentrating on calming her breathing, steadying her pulse. She turned around another landing, spotting the door at the bottom of the final flight of stairs. The light flickered again, plunging the stairs briefly into terrifying blackness.

Amy bit back a scream, plastering herself up against the wall, fingers digging into the cold, damp brickwork. She barely had time to suck in another breath before the lights came back on, a soft buzz sounding from the bulb above her head. She dashed down the final steps, almost tripping at the bottom, falling into the door with a muffled thud.

The door protested as she wrenched it open, spilling out on to the wider space of the platform. She pressed a trembling hand to her chest, leaning forward slightly as she sent a gaze around the platform. The place was deserted; no one to amuse with her panic. Amy stepped away from the stairwell, moving along the platform, looking for the electronic board that would let her know when the next train was due to arrive.

Its cheery, yellow glow told her that trains were running late due to an accident earlier that day and that her train would arrive in five minutes. Finally feeling her breathing returning to something that approached normality, Amy let her lashes fall, hiding worried, green eyes. She sucked in two slow breaths, telling herself that she was calm and cool, that the stations had stood through a war; there was no way they would suddenly collapse around her, smothering her in tile and concrete.

Her lashes fluttered up and she stared around the empty platform as she made her way over to one of the benches that huddled up against the curved wall of the station. Amy let her gaze travel up the curve of the wall, pupils contracting against the bright light that rebounded from the white tiles. The tiles coated nearly the full curve of the tunnel, leaving the far wall dark and bare, highlighting the posters that described events Amy could never afford to attend.

She sighed again, a soft breath. *Really,* she told herself, *you should be thankful. Thousands of people would kill to be in your situation. You have a roof over your head, a job, a place at nursing school. So what if you've never seen Les Mis, or that you can't afford a venti latte from Starbucks.* The ramble of her thoughts was interrupted when a soft sound came from further along the platform. The lights overhead shivered. The sound came again.

Amy rose to her feet, hands clutching tightly at her bag. She stepped towards the yellow line that marked the edge of the platform, staring along towards the dark arch through which the trains came. She tiptoed lightly along the platform, eyes wide, almost holding her breath. There it was again, a soft mewl. Something was in pain. Amy's steps quickened along the platform, hand dipping into her bag for her mobile phone, until she realised that it wouldn't work this far underground.

She was approaching the end of the platform and she looked carefully about her for the source of the noise. The soft cry came again, this time accompanied by the hitch of breath and what sounded like the flutter of wings. *Did pigeons make it this far into the stations?* Amy had seen mice down here before, their small grey bodies scurrying along the tracks, picking at the scraps that dropped down from the platforms. Maybe it was a cat or one of those urban foxes.

But pigeons didn't make that kind of mewling noise. She had no idea what kind of noise a fox made. Amy looked around, dipping her head to peer under the benches. She almost missed the small archway. It was nearly hidden behind a curved and decorated screen that edged towards the platform, but there it was. Amy approached the opening carefully, listening intently. The cry came again, a low sound laden with pain and anguish and despair.

Despite her misgivings, Amy squeezed past the carved screen and peered along the short passageway. The roof was low, the passage curving back away from the tunnel that carried the trains. There didn't seem to be any lights affixed to the passageway roof but a soft glow filtered through from the far end.

"Hello?" Amy called out gently. Perhaps one of the many homeless people had spotted the almost hidden passage and decided to hide out down here. It was warmer and drier than the streets; that had to be worth putting up with the noise and the smell of oil and diesel and overheated humanity that permeated the underground.

"Are you hurt? Do you need help?"

"Help." The sound echoed back from the passageway and Amy frowned, unable to tell if it was a response, a question or just her voice circling back to her. Another strange sound trailed its way out to her: a soft, metallic noise, as well as the shuffle of something else against stone, another mewling gasp. Amy could no longer bear the hurt sound, and she ducked her head, heading into the passageway towards that soft glow.

She followed the curve of the wall, the light of the station fading behind her, until she was bathed in the soft shimmering light ahead of her. The curved wall beside her was damp, the moisture gleaming in the faint light. The passage started to open up, widening into a small circle of a room. An oubliette. Amy had no idea where the word came from, but she knew that this was what this place was.

As she rounded the last curve of the passage, the first thing she saw was a foot, pale and fine-boned. The sole was stained dark with soot from the tunnels, darker over the ball and heel. She let her gaze track over the foot, finding the sharp bone of the ankle, a slim but muscular calf, the skin paler there, less crusted with grime and soot.

"Hello?" Her voice was so faint this time that she could barely hear herself so she called out again, slightly louder. "Hello? I just want to help. Do you need medical help? I'm a nurse, well, a trainee one, but..."

Her voice trailed away into silence as she moved forwards and finally took in the rest of the being curled on the floor of the small chamber. Another pale leg sprawled across the floor, this one curled up slightly towards the body. Pale slender arms were wrapped around a body that appeared slim but still firm with muscle. The body was wrapped in dirty fabric. It may have been ivory at some point, or possibly white, it was hard to tell now. The material draped over the man's groin before it wrapped around his slim waist and trailed up over his chest, disappearing over a shoulder.

But it wasn't the fact that there was a semi-nude male in what appeared to be a toga huddled on the floor of the small chamber that made Amy gasp and step back against the wall. Two other things had caught her attention and her mind raced as she tried to make sense of the sight in front of her.

Long chains draped down from bolts that were fastened securely into the wall of the chamber. The links were dark with age, but there was no sign of rust or wear. They attached to each of the man's wrists; wide metal cuffs forming the last link on each chain. Amy could only see the one, the other tucked against the man's chest, but they seemed to have been melted on. There was no sign of a fastener or a lock.

The second things that caught her eye were the huge wings that rose up behind the man's shoulders to drape across the floor. The feathers were tattered and bedraggled, grey with soot and dirt where they rubbed against the floor and the wall, fading to white where they neared his body.

"No, uh-uh. This is just a dream, Amy. No way is there a man with wings lying in front of you under the Islington tube station. Time to wake up and go home." The softly murmured words did nothing to break the spell.

Amy pressed herself back against the wall, sidling along the damp stonework, back towards the passageway behind her. Her hand brushed over a brick, its edge broken and sharp. She gasped as her skin parted, jerking it away from the wall to stare in dismay at the small gash that cut across her palm. Red droplets welled up, melting together in the palm of her hand.

"Ow, goddammit!"

This brought the man's head up and Amy froze, bleeding hand cradled in the other, green eyes caught in the deep sapphire gaze of the being in front of her. His hair was dark, long and tumbling around his face and jaw, brushing against cheekbones made sharper by his slenderness.

Amy found herself stepping forward as the man tilted his head to one side, hair obscuring one of those gorgeous eyes as he examined her. She felt his stare as he took in the damp, red shoes, her jeans that were once black but that had now faded to a dark grey. His head then tilted back, exposing the soft curve of his throat, the swell of his Adam's apple and he continued his slow perusal.

Amy watched as his gaze lingered on her hands, one pale, one smeared with blood. It moved up over the curve of her chest, finding the soft shadow at the base of her throat. Amy felt her pulse speed, barely resisted the urge to bring her fingers to her neck. Her red hair had started the day pulled up in a neat pony tail, but now Amy could feel damp tendrils curling against her cheeks, sticking to her skin. Finally, those dark blue eyes met hers again and Amy felt her heart stop, her breath frozen in her chest.

Long lashes fluttered slightly and time seemed to restart, Amy jerking forward another step towards the man, towards the angel? His wings rustled, feathers twitching against the floor of the small room, the arches at the top opening out as he tried to flex them. Another soft cry of pain and loss and desperation slipped from between his lips.

Amy dropped to her knees beside him, hand reaching out in an automatic need to soothe and comfort. Her fingers made contact with the pale skin just above the manacle and the lights fluttered around them. Amy looked up towards the ceiling, searching for the source of the light but the plastered roof was bare. It was then that Amy realised the source of the soft glow was the being in front of her.

She brushed her fingers lightly over the delicate skin of his inner arm and saw a shiver run across the pale skin.

"Hi, I'm Amy. I just want to help. Is there anything I can do? Who chained you up here? Are you hurt? Hungry? Thirsty? I have some water I think, in my bag."

Amy sat back on her heels, searching in her bag for the bottle of water. She found it, unscrewed the lid and held it out to the angel. He stared at her, still silent and Amy leant closer, patting gently at one pale calf as she held the water out.

"It's just water. I opened it this morning, so it's fresh." The angel moaned, a shudder running through him, his eyes closing in what was either pain or pleasure. He opened his eyes and fixed them on where Amy's hand rested on his leg. She glanced down and pulled her hand back with a gasped apology. Her hand flew up to her mouth as she saw the red smear of blood across his pale skin.

"Oh shit, I'm so sorry. I'll just get a tissue, wipe that off. Is it okay if I touch you? Just to clean that up?" Amy grabbed a packet of tissues from her bag pulling them out of the plastic wrapping, making a pad with a couple. She pressed that against her palm before dampening another with some of the water.

Her gaze moved back to the angel's leg just in time to see him trail his slender fingers through the blood she had smeared on him. He stared at his stained fingers before he slid them slowly into his mouth, a pale pink tongue flickering out to lick slowly at his own skin, lapping at them until they were devoid of blood.

"You... you..." Amy stuttered and then let out a soft cry when his hand lashed out, the chain rattling and clinking wildly as his hand wrapped tightly around her wrist, pulling her injured hand towards him. He plucked at the tissue, discarding the scrunched bundle with a delicate crinkle of his nose. His gaze fixed on the cut that trailed over the fleshy mound beneath her thumb.

He squeezed at her hand, a rhythmic clenching that made the flesh part, blood welling in small droplets again. His gaze came up to meet hers as he pulled her hand closer, tipping his head down as he stared up through his lashes. His tongue came out, pressing gently on her skin, before he curled it over her palm, licking away the smudges.

He pulled at Amy again and she fell forward against him, her right hand coming to rest on his thigh, her face level with his collarbone. He shifted his grip, tipping her hand until he could fit his mouth over her left palm. He sucked hard at the flesh, tongue working at the cut in kittenish laps. Amy moaned softly at the strange sensation, feeling his skin heat beneath her.

"What are you... oh god..." Amy's voice trailed off again on a gasp as the angel moved his mouth from her palm, pushing at the sleeve of her top to get to the soft skin of her wrist. A frustrated growl rumbled out of him and he tugged at her clothing, lips pushing out into a pout.

Chapter 2
Freedom's Cost

Amy tried to struggle away but the angel's grip hardened around her wrist. She could feel the bones grate together as his fingers shifted around the joint. His other hand tugged at her coat, pulling it down one arm, her bag sliding from her shoulder and falling to the floor, contents spilling across the damp concrete.

She struggled, tugging at her arm but the angel shifted up on to his knees, wings flaring out behind him. The feathers made a sound like tearing silk as they brushed over the floor, the chains shifting and clinking. He grabbed for her bare arm, long fingers wrapping around the lower part of the limb, digging into the flesh, pushing against the bone.

"Ow, please. No, that hurts!" Amy cried out, tears welling up as she continued to try and pull away. Another growl rumbled out of the angel as he pulled at her coat, ripping it from her other arm. Goosebumps chased up her flesh, the air damp and chill in the small, stone room. A wing tip flicked the discarded coat away and the angel wrapped his free hand around the soft swell of her upper arm, the hand that was round her wrist sliding up to grip her other arm.

Amy could see the circlet of red marks around her wrist, knew that by tomorrow it would have blossomed into hues of purple and blue-red. As his fingers gripped her biceps she could feel more bruises forming and she kicked out, a foot making contact with his thigh.

"Let me go! Fucker! Someone will hear, I'll scream." Amy paused to haul in a breath, hoping that someone would have come down for the last train. The floor began to vibrate and Amy's scream was lost in the sound of the train's brakes as it pulled into the station.

The angel rose to his feet, wings towering behind him. He pulled Amy in, wrapping a length of chain around her waist, tying her to him. He pulled at her t-shirt, until the stitching gave way and the material pooled at her waist. He paused, blue eyes raking over the expanse of skin exposed to him.

His left hand slid round behind Amy, fingers spreading wide over her spine, his legs shifting until she was cradled between his thighs. Tears spilling over her lashes, Amy shook her head, "No, don't! Please, please, I don't want to... don't want to..."

A hand curled into her hair, slipping the band from her ponytail, fingers weaving into the fallen strands as Amy shook her head in denial. The fingers tightened, pulling her head to the side so that the angel could bury his mouth in the curve of her neck, mouthing at her pulse point, biting and licking at the skin.

Amy continued to plead as the angel sucked bruise after bruise into the tender skin along her collarbones, nosing at the hollow of her throat, licking down into the valley of her cleavage. "Please. Aren't you an angel? Why are you doing this? Please, let me go. I haven't... I don't..." The angel closed a hand over a breast, fingers slipping beneath the material of her bra to nudge at her nipple. A soft sigh slipped from him and he rocked his hips up against Amy.

Amy brought up her hand, resting it against the angel's face, trying to bring the angel's attention to hers, her green eyes wet with tears, cheeks flushed with shame. The angel simply tilted his head in an odd, birdlike fashion and stared at her, eyes devoid of emotion, before leaning in to lick at the salt trails. Amy let her lashes slip down as the angel lapped at her face, licking at her mouth in a parody of a kiss.

The world swirled around her and suddenly Amy found herself pinned, her back against the wall, chains cold against her upper back where they crossed behind her. The angel slipped a knee between her thighs, pushing her legs apart. His fingers slipped down over the skin of her stomach, the flesh contracting at the ticklish touch. He kept one hand against her chest, pressed between her breasts, pinning her to the wall. The other worked at her belt, the button and zip of her jeans.

Tears spilled out of Amy's eyes again as she felt her jeans slipping down over her thighs. Her cheeks flushed deep rose as she tried to bring her legs together. The angel crouched in front of her, soft breath chasing over the sensitive skin of her stomach as he finished removing her jeans. He slid back up, mouth trailing over her skin, tongue flickering out to taste her.

Amy closed her eyes, tried to disappear inside herself as she felt her underwear fall away. The angel's hands slid across her skin, his fingers warm on her chilled flesh. He dipped his head again, nuzzling into the curve of her neck as he slipped one heated digit inside her. He moaned with delight as he found the evidence of her purity, not that he had needed it.

Amy's pleas had exposed her purity, and she wondered that the angel seemed to react even more intently, seemed pleased that she was untouched. He continued to nuzzle at her, biting and marking her, rubbing his scent all over her. Amy's pleas turned to gasps as the angel continued to work his finger inside her, slipping another one in, pushing at her inner walls.

He stopped moving and Amy held her breath for a moment before letting her eyes open. She looked up at the angel, watched as he slid his fingers into his mouth again, blue eyes gleaming, skin glowing as he tasted her on his fingers. He stared into her eyes as he moved his hands down to her thighs.

"Please, don't..." The plea was barely a whisper. The angel just tilted his head again and blinked slowly at her.

Wrapping his fingers underneath the curves of her ass, he flexed his muscles and Amy was lifted off her feet, pushed up against the wall as he wrapped her legs around his waist, thrusting into her in one long glide. The chill of the wall pressing against her back, the rough texture of the stone, could not distract her from the stabbing hurt that spread through her pelvis. Amy let out a long, pained wail, hands thumping against his shoulders. The angel ignored her protest, pulling his hips back and pushing up and in again. The sharp pain dulled into a low throbbing ache, pulsing inside her with each beat of her heart, swelling in waves with each slow jerk of his hips.

He continued the slow, steady movement, grinding into her at the end of each deep push, scraping her skin against the wall, licking at the tears that continued to spill down her cheeks. He slipped a hand free, Amy's leg drooping towards the floor. It changed the angle of his movement inside her and Amy cried out as a new sensation fluttered through her stomach.

The angel purred, biting at her throat, his fingers entwining into her hair again, pulling at it, tipping her head back. His hand traced the blossoming necklace of bruises, pushing against the tortured skin, watching Amy wince at the pain he caused her. She swallowed her cries, tears continuing in silence.

He curled his body, wings spreading wide, as he dipped his head to her breasts, sinking his teeth hard into the tender flesh, sucking at the nipples until they pebbled hard and rosy pink. He slowed his movement, grinding his hips against Amy's for a long moment before he pulled nearly all the way out, the head of his cock lingering at her entrance. For a long moment she wondered if he was going to stop, to let her go. Maybe her lack of response wasn't what he wanted. She held her breath, a soft prayer running through her mind.

The breath stuttered out of her as he closed his fingers around Amy's throat, tipping her head up so that he could stare into her eyes. Amy tried to tilt her head away, hiding behind her lashes, but the angel tightened his grip, cutting off her air until she met his gaze. Slowly his lips curved and then he shoved forward, pistoning into her, thrusting her against the wall, hips crashing into the cradle of her pelvis, trapping her between the hard chill of the concrete and the warm solidity of his flesh.

Amy cried out, unable to hold it back, her soft moans and gasps filling the small room, drowning out the wet sounds of flesh sliding into flesh. The angel continued to lick at her tears, hand cradling her throat, the other still holding one thigh up around his hip until he came, spilling into her hot and wet and deep. Amy felt him pulse deep within her and her head drooped as he removed his hand from her throat. Pain shuddered through Amy from her scraped back, her bruised neck and arms, that soft place between her thighs. She collapsed against the wall as the angel dropped to his knees in front of her, hands spreading wide over the bones of her hips, cradling her pelvis.

Amy's eyes flew open, her mouth rounding into a soft 'o' of surprise as the angel buried his head between her legs, nuzzling at her mons. She tried to clench her thighs together but the angel dug cruel fingers into her hips, pinching at the nerves, until she went limp against the wall. His hands tilted her hips forward and his tongue flickered out, licking into her, lapping away the traces of blood and semen that trickled out of her. He continued to lick at her, nipping at the skin of her inner thighs, teeth threatening pain each time she tried to wriggle away, his thumbs rubbing along the crease where thigh met pelvis.

He blew softly over her skin and Amy shuddered, a soft moan slipping from her bitten lips. She stuck her hand into her mouth to silence herself as the angel returned to his avid attentions. Amy could feel something building low in her stomach, her hips jerking against her will towards the angel's face as he licked and sucked at her most secret place.

The angel slowly slid two fingers back inside of her, twisting and rubbing them inside her, dragging them slowly over her as he fluttered his tongue against her clitoris. Amy's hand flew from the wall, where it had been pressed for so long and she curled her fingers hard into the tumble of dark waves at the back of his head. She was going to pull him away, she was, just as soon as... as soon as...

The angel moaned against her, lips curving and he pushed his mouth up against her, the faintest scrape of teeth as he licked hard. Amy felt her muscles tighten, her toes curling against the floor as her orgasm rippled through her. A low wail echoed round the room and Amy realised it was her. Her legs buckled and the angel let her slip slowly down the wall to sprawl naked on the damp concrete.

He shifted round behind her, untangling the chains so they once more hung loose between wall and wrist. He pulled Amy on to his lap, nuzzling once more into her neck, his fingers working at her nipples. As her pulse began to slow he slipped one hand down again, over the soft curve of her stomach, slicking his fingers through the wetness between her thighs.

He smeared the moisture over her own mouth, her lips parting laxly to let him slip his fingers in, trailing them over her tongue and teeth. He lifted her slightly and she felt the head of his cock nudge at her again. She shuddered and shook her head slightly, but she was all out of fight, confused and bewildered and hurting, her mind curled up inside her skull, leaving her body to the angel. Amy heard him purr lowly behind her, his mouth nipping at her ear and then he was lowering her slowly down, his hard shaft sliding back inside her, slipping easily through the slick of saliva and her own dampness.

The new position allowed him to rock his hips into her, his cock sliding against her inner walls. Amy squirmed on his lap, keening as she felt him slide lower down the wall behind them, his hips curving up higher, thrusting further into her. She felt the faint tickle as he trailed one hand back up to her mouth and she licked at his intruding fingers, circling her tongue around the digits, her lips bruised red and swollen. He seemed to like that, humming into the back of her neck.

She watched absently as his hand worked back down her body, pausing to pinch at each taut nipple, nails digging into each tender mound of flesh. Amy wriggled against him, pulling more low purrs from the angel behind her, the sound vibrating through them. His hand continued downwards, slipping between her thighs.

The angel let his own knees fall outwards, forcing Amy's legs apart, exposing her to the cool air. Her face heated at the thought of the image they made, sprawled on the bare stone, his fingers tracing round the place where they were joined, her head tipped back on his shoulder as he bit and sucked at her neck.

His fingers worked her slowly and carefully as he continued to rock inside her, the tension building in Amy again as she felt his flesh harden within her, the muscles in his arms tightening around her. Amy began to rock against him, her body seeking the pleasure his touches were promising, grinding back into his lap, pushing up towards his teasing fingers. The angel built the tension higher and higher in her until she was keening almost constantly, her hips rocking frantically, soft pleas dropping from her lips in a scratched and broken voice.

He thrust hard, sliding a finger in beside his swollen cock and Amy screamed as the tension released, her body flooding with pleasure. The world swirled around her and faded slowly to black. The angel smiled and thrust once more, coming hard inside her. He slipped out of her, replacing his cock with his fingers, slicking them in the mix of their fluids. He brought the glistening fingers to each shackle, smearing the moisture across the gleaming bands.

There was a soft chime and the metal darkened and cracked, crumbling around his wrists, falling to the floor in soft piles of ash.

The angel rubbed at his wrists, letting Amy slide off his lap, leaving her curled on the floor. Wings curled tight around his body he slipped through the passageway, disappearing into the blackness of the subway tunnel.

Amy came to, shivering on the cold, stone floor. She winced as she pulled herself up, feeling moisture trickle down her thighs. She wiped herself with the remains of the tissues, balling them up. She stared at the crumpled bundle, unsure what to do with it. She dropped them on the floor and dragged her underwear and jeans over her bruised thighs. Her t-shirt was beyond redemption so she stuffed it into her bag, adding the tissues to the crumpled mess, unwilling to leave any evidence of what had happened. She pulled her coat on, zipping it up high to hide the bare flesh, the bruises that were blooming across her skin.

Limping, she dragged herself back to the tube station, pulling herself up the stairs. A low rumble had come from the tunnel as she entered the stairwell, the walls vibrating, but this time she didn't care if the walls fell in. Amy finally made it up the stairs, exiting the station. A police man rushed over to her as she came out.

"Miss! What were you doing in there? Didn't you hear?"

"Train. I was waiting, the train..."

The police man wrapped a gentle hand around her arm, Amy trying not to wince as he made contact with the bruises hidden beneath her coat as he shepherded her off to one side.

"There was an abandoned tube station, the next one on the line, City Road?"

Amy nodded vaguely even though she hadn't heard of it.

"It just exploded. People say that a bright, white light just flew out of the ground. Dunno what they were storing down there. Used to be a bomb shelter during the war you know."

Amy nodded again.

"Huge bang, the brightest light you ever did see," the policeman continued.

"Angel," murmured Amy. "There was an angel."

"Yeah, the Angel Islington, that's where you are darlin'. You bump your head? Come on, we'll get you an ambulance, get you checked over. Didn't know there were still folk down there. You see anyone else down there?"

"No, no one else."

If you enjoyed this story, you can sign up for a free membership at
ForbiddenFiction and discuss it with other readers
and the author at the *Underneath It All* story page
at http://forbiddenfiction.com/library/story/KM1-1.000024.

Devilish Trick

L.D. Durham

After taking a two-decade hiatus after writing her first book in first grade, L.D. Durham has been writing for others for nearly ten years. Her beginnings in fanfiction taught her many ways to titillate and entertain readers, along with smoothing out the mechanics of writing a good story. Having taken her training wheels off, she has published two books and wrote original, serial fiction for four years.

Chapter 1
The Deal

It's funny how humans paint pictures of Heaven and Hell and its natives. This has always been a fascination for me. I love reading the books and watching the movies; the deadly battles between serpent-like demons and the effervescent angels. Human notions can be brilliant and silly at the exact same time. In reality, truth, as often is the case, is much more lackluster.

If you've never been to Heaven before, or if you don't remember, it's really just a big family dinner. Honestly, who enjoys those? The Great Fall was just one of those family dinners gone terribly wrong. Cousin Luke got a bit drunk and had some of his brothers and cousins with him, backing him up. He thought he knew what he was talking about when he rambled on and on. And on. (Luke has always been quite long-winded about his ideas on what is correct and what isn't.) Father, the host, disagreed and, finally, told them all to get out. Now two sides of the family rarely talk to each other and when they do, it's all sniping and one-upping each other. A great big game. Throughout it all, there have been intermediaries who talk with both sides, trying to make reconciliation happen.

And then you have me.

I'm just your simple, nosy busybody who wants in on all the gossip. Some, unjustly, call me spy, while others call me informant, as if there is a difference between the two. And there are others who call me a nasty little twerp who must have his finger in everyone's pie. In fact, one was calling me such a thing at that very moment. I laughed. "I love the way you demons turn a phrase. You make it all so... dirty."

Marbas raised an eyebrow at me before flicking his cigarette away. "An angel titillated by dirtiness. What is Heaven coming to?"

Grinning, I said, "I wouldn't know. I haven't been up There in quite a while."

"Next you'll be producing Nephilim." Marbas smirked. "Actually, do that, will you?"

"I've never been particularly drawn to human women, so I doubt I would ever do such a thing as impregnate them even if I were to fall, thank you very much." Actually, the idea horrified me, as he knew it would. But I kept my cool. He could talk about bad angels and their actions all he wanted. He certainly had authority, after all. Speaking with demons was always a bit thrilling for that, alone.

He pushed away from the block wall I had found him leaning against and started to walk away. The alley we were in was between a library and a closed print shop. The library's windows were dingy and only cast minimal light into our space, but I could still easily make out my retreating companion. Marbas appeared exactly as a human would expect a demon to look like in man-skin: black hair in a crazy young hairstyle, a bit of stubble shadowing his jaw, nearly glow-in-the-dark light blue eyes, and muscular. A good girl or boy's erotic fantasy of a bad boy. Ironically, it was exactly what he had looked like when strutting about Heaven.

Well, he didn't have the stubble back then.

I leapt down from the wall that had hidden an empty garbage tip, and followed after him. "And who will you be corrupting tonight?"

He stopped and looked at me out of the corner of his eye. "Go away, angel. You're annoying me."

"And here I thought I was supposed to bring one comfort and enlightenment."

"You're trying to steal my fleshbag. Now buzz off." He started back down the alleyway. It was nearly pitch-black in the alleyway, but, hey, we're supernatural beings. We don't need light.

"Saving, damning. It's just a score card," I said. A reader may think I am being quite casual about a topic so important to humans. But I have to say that in the grand scheme of things, in the hundreds of years, off and on, I have spent with humans, most usually do just fine on their own and don't need a lot of help. Which is probably why

I spend a lot of time among them: it's a fairly easy gig. However, it can get a bit tedious living among beings that don't often see you for who you really are. (There was the one time I appeared in the smears on Mrs. Norris's living room window, but I got a reprimand on my record for it. I admit it was worth it, though.) It's why I liked finding and interacting with demons. It made me feel a bit like an archangel, except I'd look ridiculous with a sword and I could never pull off the posturing. But demons don't find me a threat that needs reviling, and I don't find them repellent. In fact, I quite enjoyed pestering Marbas, in particular, even though he's one of the higher-ups and isn't interested in gossip.

I grabbed Marbas' defined and muscular arm, half covered by a tight short-sleeve shirt, and tugged him to a stop, which he had to allow for it to work. I'm much smaller than Marbas. Always have been. I prefer to think of my size as the best kind there is for being non-threatening and good for working with children. In fact, I've been referred to as being as cute as a Cherub by some humans I've worked with. Which, in all honesty, can be a bit confusing since I'm not sure if they mean the relatively modern version of a toddler with wings, or the original version with four heads. I don't have four heads, by the way. And though I may be a little soft and not a hard-bodied warrior, I don't resemble a toddler either. If I were to guess, I would say most humans might say I look like a fairly attractive brunet man in his mid-twenties who appears to still be in college. (In other words, I enjoy comfortable, loose clothes. If you haven't yet worn a sweatshirt, may I add I believe them to be divine?) Humans may even say I have a compelling personality, which is a good tool for the job. Either way, I generally take it to mean that I am adorable and sweet, which is perfect for my function of helping humans out. That, and I've tried for eons to change it and can't. Apparently, the Almighty likes me just as I am. Bugger.

"If you tell me what your plans are tonight, I'll let you in on Gabriel's big scheme for two years from now," I said, cajolingly, still holding Marbas' beefy arm. "Think of the feather in your cap that would be, if you thwarted him. There are sick orphans involved," I sang.

"Not interested."

"Fine. I'll tell you about the scandalous secret that Apollyon is trying to keep hush-hush."

Marbas turned to face me. "Still not interested."

I scrunched up my face and pouted. "I'm just curious about what you are doing. I am willing to make a fair trade for the information."

He eyed me a moment. I smiled and in the side-dimension that we can see at all times but humans don't (actually, some humans do, but then other humans often put them in locked hospitals soon after), I lifted my wings up. My wings appeared in all their glorious, pale white featheriness. Ok, well, they could have been a bit brighter and fuller, but like I said, I'm not the greatest of angels. I have some issues with authority and my superior says I may have a smidge of daring. He's says this while frowning.

With my ethereal wings aloft, I attempted to look as innocent and earnest as I could. I'd have slipped on my halo if I knew it wouldn't have pissed him off. Demons, generally, had been fine with their wings losing their feathers. It was the loss of the halos that really stung. Something to do with making their hair look good, I think.

"Fine, angel. Here's the deal," Marbas said, in a voice that would have terrified a human. However, I've heard it before. The intimidation factor just isn't there any longer. "I tell you what is going down tonight. Afterwards, I get any one thing in your power to give me."

This, if you haven't noticed, is a deal with a devil. One must tread carefully here.

"I am intrinsically unable to harm others in any capacity," I reminded him.

"Yeah, I know that." He had the look of someone who knew he was reeling in a big one.

"And material goods I can create turn to dust in three hours."

"Don't annoy me. What do I need with ephemeral junk?" he snorted.

I narrowed my eyes at him, thinking hard. But only for a moment. I really wanted to know, and I did enjoy hanging out with Marbas, especially when he knew I was there and was speaking to me.

"All right, I agree."

Alas, there is a reason I am not a top-ranking angel. I'm not as clever and all-knowing as the Seraphim, and I am certainly only a speck of dust compared to the Hayot. I'm bottom of the barrel. The

Heavenly Host is tens of thousands and I am quite forgotten about and rarely called to do more than I do, which is not a whole lot. I suspect I would have fallen already if I didn't think the other side would actually make me work.

Marbas smiled. "Deal. And I'll even be magnanimous. I'll let you tag along tonight."

"Really?" I smiled. "Thank you."

"Don't mention it." He leaned in, his face serious. "Really, don't mention it."

"Understood," I said with a nod.

He took me down the street a bit to a busy little bar. It was upper-scale, but not top class. A place where a-bit-better-off-than-others stopped in for a drink before heading home to their slightly-larger-than-others' houses.

"Heya, Mark, how's it going?" a man called from a small table near the wall. Marbas returned the happy greeting and made his way toward the man. I paused for a moment, not sure what to do. Marbas hadn't said I shouldn't be seen, so I stayed in corporeal form, minus the wings, and hurried to catch up. I was wading through the people when a tipsy woman knocked her purse off a table and I grabbed it for her before it spilled out. As she thanked me, I touched her shoulder and helped sober her a bit. I also reminded her of her mother's birthday. As I continued across, I heard her tell her friends good-bye and ask where the closest florist was.

See? I do my job, as small and sporadic as it is. Everyone needs those moments of help in keeping good relationships and avoiding accidents or finding their keys immediately when there is an emergency. Just call me the Angel of Tiny Mercies.

"Your friend?" the man at the table asked as I walked up.

Marbas nodded. "Yeah. Old school friend, named Clarence. Clarence, this is Don."

Clarence? I assure you I was no Clarence and Marbas was no Jimmy Stewart. Demons needed to update their joke catalog. I grimaced at him for the name he gave me, then smiled at Don. "Hello, nice to meet you."

Don shook my hand and I could feel the sadness in him. It was soul-deep.

"Clarence is a psychologist," Marbas added as I sat down. "I thought he could help you out."

"Really?" Don seemed nervous and glanced between us. "Did you tell him... what's going on?"

"I wouldn't betray a confidence, Don. You know that." Marbas seemed both caring and a bit hurt. Really well-played.

"I will do anything I can to help," I said, with real feeling. I'm made of help, actually. Kind of goes with the wings, no matter how soiled they get.

Don again glanced nervously around before sighing. "I've been... thinking about having an affair. I have a co-worker." He paused. "She's really nice and sweet. We've... we've kissed a couple of times." He looked up at me. "But, I'm married. For eight years. Angela and I," he sighed, "we were in love, but it just seems like she can't stand me anymore. We fight all the time. But, the kids. We can't let them see us fighting. And we can't split them up, you know?" He shook his head and lowered it again. "But Sarah is just..." He sighed, again, heavily. "I don't know what I should do anymore."

Adultery really wasn't my normal bag. It's one of those big ones usually handled by an angel above my pay grade who specializes in emotions, current cultural morality, and all that. But I couldn't sit by and not do something.

"You gotta do what feels right," Marbas said quietly. "You only live once."

"Yes, but living it while feeling guilt and remorse is not the way to do it," I spoke up. I leaned forward, placing my hands on the table. "Don, I think you still love your wife. Marriage isn't perfect. It can't be. You—we are only human and humans squabble and fight and have bad days. Even bad months. Or years. But that doesn't mean it can't get better. Sarah sounds like a great woman, but is it fair to put her in that situation? To make her the other woman?"

Don sighed again and shook his head.

"Go to your wife," I urged. "Talk to her. Tell her how you feel. Tell her how much you love her and miss her. I'm sure things will get better. And you can let Sarah find her own untangled happiness."

He sat there for a moment, then looked up at Marbas. "What do you think?"

"I think Clarence is speaking good words," Marbas said, looking as though he was in deep thought.

Don nodded again, then stood up, downing his drink. "Yeah. Yeah, you're right." He straightened his shoulders and held his hand out to me. We shook and I could feel his determination and renewed hope. I smiled up at him.

"Good luck," I said.

"Thank you. Thank you, both."

We watched him stride out of the bar.

Marbas leaned back in his chair and drank from a glass I hadn't seen show up on the table. "Good work, angel. You just prevented him from committing adultery."

I looked at him and smiled. "And thwarted you from making him do it," I said proudly. "You shouldn't have had me tag along."

Marbas grinned. "Actually, I came here to talk him out of the affair, too."

My face kind of froze. "Huh?"

"You see, his wife wants out of the marriage. Badly. She wants to sell everything, get the cash, and pay back her gambling debts. She's been pushing Sarah in his face for a while now. She wants him to cheat, so she can get the divorce and guilt him into giving her most of everything." Marbas took another drink, his eyes dancing over the rim of the glass at me. "Now, she'll be desperate after he comes home to confess his renewed love for her. I expect dear Don will be having an 'accident' soon. He's worth quite a lot dead, you know."

I sat there, staring at him. I blinked a couple of times and my mouth opened once or twice as I tried to think of something to say. Marbas chuckled and leaned over to me.

"Thanks, angel. You helped me out quite a bit. I've been after the wife for a few months." He kissed my temple and stood up. "Now, shall we go?"

I blindly got to my feet, still flummoxed at the neat turn I had just been given. "Where?"

"To my humble abode where I shall now take what you have the power to give me." He smiled down at me, a devil's smile, a demon's grin. "Your heavenly body."

Chapter 2
The Collection

How many times must we be warned not to make deals with devils? But we always think, *No, no. I've got this. I've seen all the movies and read up on it. No way is a devil going to outsmart me.* And really, I should have known better, because I know all that thinking is just rubbish.

And yet, there I was being smiled at by a demon...

...in a very nice apartment, I feel I must point out. Much nicer than anything I had ever stayed in. I was currently standing in an overly-spacious living room with black walls and beige furniture. The floor was white stone. There were several expensive curios on glass shelves being lit by beautifully subtle lighting in the ceiling. The apartment even had a skyline view! Maybe the other side does pay better.

"You've been toddling after me for a few years now," Marbas said, breaking me out of thoughts of a career move. His silhouette moved across the floor-to-ceiling windows. The lights from the city below were the main illumination in the room and they cast him in shadow. His eyes glinted as he turned his head from the view and looked in my direction. "Is this what you wanted?"

I decided to prevaricate, as I tried working out how to get things back in control. "An apartment this large on this side of the city? I should say so. But I don't think you're going to give it to me." I pointedly looked at the skyline. "With that view, you must have had to damn someone quite important to get this."

"He's letting me borrow it while he takes care of some 'investments' I helped him think about." Marbas walked toward me, so I casually stepped back and around the incredibly too-plush sofa. He stopped and grinned at me. "But I wasn't talking about the apartment, was I? How long have you fancied me, angel?"

"I don't fancy you!" I made gasping noises of outrage, which, of course, made me look guilty. So I immediately stopped and tried to act casual, putting my hand down and leaning on the back of the sofa. Marbas interested me, sure. And, yes, I usually stuck around to areas I knew he haunted. Maybe I watched him from afar, okay? Possibly I asked after him if he had been away from the mortal plane for a while. I already mentioned I found him stimulating, but in a very off-hand, casual, hardly interested kind of way, obviously. I'd hardly call watching him, trying to talk to him whenever I could, and being generally interested in his whereabouts at all times anything like fancying him. So I clearly told him this. "You're just something to break up the boredom. It's a bit spare in entertainment down here sometimes, you know?"

"And lonely." Marbas stared hard at me from across the furniture. "I hear that you've been sent here on your own to try to toughen you up a bit. You're alone in this town." He put one knee on the sofa and was only a few inches away from me. "Did you come looking for company? Did you come looking for another of your kind to alleviate the loneliness?"

"First of all, devil, you are not of my kind."

His right eyebrow quirked up. "Oh, getting prissy now, are we?"

"And secondly, I don't need toughening up. Your sources are obviously unsound." I smirked at him. "You would think a demon of your status would be better informed." I turned to walk away, but my wrist was grabbed. I'm accustomed, after all these years, to having human emotions bleed onto me. Any touch of the flesh without it is a bit disconcerting and being touched by any kind of angel, fallen or not, has no emotion to it, leaving only the feeling of touch to focus on. That would be the disconcerting part. I yanked at my arm, but his grasp did not loosen. Did I say no emotion was disconcerting? I spoke too soon. Being held by a devil is disconcerting.

"You're afraid now," he said quietly.

I laughed. "I'm not frightened. Why should I be? You can't kill me or harm me."

"Kill? No. Harm?" He tugged on my wrist and I stumbled toward him, my hip hitting the back of the sofa. "I could do some harm if I wanted to."

"But you won't." I swallowed nervously, trying to not let him see. "You'll only start another feud. They only need one little thing to get started and battles are so annoying."

"But entertaining. You did mention being bored."

I looked down at him with wide eyes, not able to hide my concern at possibly being a bone of contention between the families. We were currently in a cold war, both sides going about their plans, talking about each other behind backs. Any act of violence between us would start outright war back up again, and that really messes with humans. It had only been quiet since just before the middle of the last century. I couldn't imagine being the catalyst for it all starting again so soon.

He grinned evilly. If you've never seen a devil grin, you've never seen an evil grin. It drips with condescension, glee, and poison.

"What's the matter, angel? I thought you weren't frightened? I just want to taste heavenly flesh tonight. We made a deal."

"And I will honor it."

"Of course you will," he agreed nicely, which wasn't nice at all, actually. "Breaking a deal is enough to tip you off the clouds, hmm?"

I glared at him and tugged again at my arm to be free. I was, therefore, quite shocked when I was not released, and instead was pulled over the back of the sofa. I fell onto his lap, stunned.

"There we are. This is much better, isn't it?"

"No, it isn't!" I struggled. "Unhand me!"

"Your vernacular is slipping back a century or two."

"I don't care." I scrambled to get off of him, pulling at his arms. I am sure he was using many more than two hands. If I wasn't in such a fluster, I might have stopped to count. It's unfortunate that striking out at him did not occur to me. But, I am only a helper angel, after all. No matter how loosely I fit the bill, violence just isn't in my repertoire. Who do I look like? Michael?

In an embarrassingly short amount of time, his hands (however many there were) clamped down and held me still. "You promised, angel." And I was being kissed.

I've been kissed before. By humans and by other angels. Most have been pleasant, some have been unpleasant. Some have been heated and passionate and some have been platonic and brotherly.

Demons do not do pleasant, heated, passionate, or brotherly. I was engulfed in licentious sex. His mouth opened mine, his tongue plundered and controlled, rolling around in my mouth like he owned it. His lips burned, his hands burned where they touched my body. I became aware of my body. All of it. Even the bits that painters like to leave off us on their pretty canvases. If I had been wearing a fig leaf, it would have burst into flames and disintegrated. (Humans became prudes when it came to us centuries back. I'm not sure why they suddenly got missish about our nether regions, but I assure you, we had them first.)

Marbas pulled back and smiled. I tried desperately to breathe and get my body back under control. "You like that, angel? Want some more?"

I shook my head weakly, staring up into his eyes in a bit of a muddle. The idea that I had clearly bitten off much more than I could chew was scratching away at the inside of my brain, trying to get past the shock that was running around rampant in there.

"That's too bad. Because there is so much more to come."

I shook my head no. He smiled and nodded before diving down for my mouth again. I was overcome once more. Though it may be obvious, I must confess my relative inexperience with situations of a carnal nature. Being of the angelic host, I do not come with the need to breed. My body, my spirit, is not infused with desire as humans feel it. I do not randomly have erotic thoughts, nor do I feel anxious for sex.

However.

However, I am still a creature of this world. I walk both in it and beside it. I have the sense of touch. I have the sense of pleasure. And, as most creatures do, I enjoy pleasure.

And I was enjoying the pleasing touch of the devil whose lap I was currently writhing in.

"St-stop!" I gasped out as my lips were released. I could feel his hands touching me and fumbling with my clothes, though my head was having a hard time keeping track of my environment and the overwhelming sensations Marbas was creating with his mouth.

"You're not backing out of the deal, are you?"

I could feel cool air touching places that it hadn't before. "Why is my chest bare?"

"Because that's a pretty big offense. What would your superiors say?"

"Don't pinch there."

"They wouldn't be able to trust you. How could they?"

"Don't unzip that."

"You knew who you were making the deal with. If you don't even have the balls, as nice a set as these are—"

"Let those go!"

"—to pay the piper when you lose out, how can they ever trust you again? You might as well strip your wings."

"No!"

"No?"

I was nearly completely undressed, my shirt gone, my pants down to my thighs. Panting, I shook my head, holding his wrist, trying to keep his hand immobile. Why did he have such thick wrists? I had to use both hands on one of them. It could make one feel inferior.

"No, I'm not reneging. I just... I don't understand why you..." I shook my head again, trying to make sense of my thoughts. His devil grin was not making that easy.

"Are you overwhelmed? A bit besieged by your passion?"

"You don't have to do this."

"Do what?"

I looked at my naked body and licked my swollen lips. "You don't need to... to..."

"You *are* overwhelmed," he said happily. "Look at you, angel. You are the picture of lust and debauchery." A mirror appeared above us and he was right. A part of me saw how very pornographic we appeared. Another part was too swept up to make much sense at all.

I banished the mirror and once again tried to get away. And once again I was thwarted. He pushed me down onto my back and forced his way between my thighs.

"You're naked!"

"Just as I was made, even." Marbas grinned and leaned over me. "Now, let's see how you taste in other places."

He sucked at my neck. I have seen humans do this and always considered it a strange behavior of theirs. But having it done to my own neck made me realize what all the fuss was about. I shivered and he chuckled just before moving further down.

"Holy Host!" I shouted and my back arched.

"Nipples aren't just for decoration," he murmured from my chest. "But yours are pretty damn sensitive. You angels should live it up more."

I wanted to argue back. I did. I was supposed to, even. But at that moment I just couldn't figure out how my mouth worked. It just gaped open and allowed me to pant. My legs writhed, brushing against his hips, giving me more tactile pleasure. When did my trousers disappear?

"And here we have the prettiest prick I've come across." Marbas looked up from between my thighs. "Thank me, angel. I just gave you the greatest of compliments."

"Th-thank you," I gasped out. I said it automatically not really thinking of it, not really understanding what was happening to me. I'd never had my body blank out my mind before. It would have been unsettling if I could have thought about it.

"You're all revved up, but we need your dick to join the party."

"My... Ahhh!" White-hot heat engulfed a part of my anatomy I rarely thought about. But it eclipsed everything just then. My hands flailed until they latched onto Marbas' shoulders, raking and gripping them. My feet dug into the cushions, pushing my entire being into his mouth. The sucking sounds coming from him were vulgar and egged me on to greater heights. My wings broke through and appeared, so great was my fervor. One spread over the coffee table and one was squashed up against the back of the couch. Two feathers fell softly onto my arm. I decided to believe it was merely rough treatment, not my skidding down the Angel Hill that caused it. As it was, I wasn't sure I could stop wallowing in my debauchery if Lucifer himself appeared to stamp my passport.

And then he stopped.

"No! No, don't!" I gasped. I gripped his shoulders, trying to force him back down. He chuckled and rose up onto his knees. I heard a scraping sound as the delicate coffee table beside us went skidding across the floor with a wave of his hand.

"I need more room than this," he said with a leer. He wrapped his arms around my waist and lifted me up against him. I shamelessly rubbed against his stomach; the pleasure I had found was too strong to be forgotten. Marbas kissed me hard as he went down on the floor and pulled me on top of him.

"Ready for this, angel?" he asked, gripping his male organ and pumping it through his fist a few times. I had heard that demons hid their tails in their penis. I may have found proof. It was larger, thicker than a human's but not freakishly so. I started to go down in order to use my mouth as he had done, thinking I could return to the pleasure if I did. He stopped me and pulled me up to lay on his chest.

"Spread your legs. Straddle me."

"Are we going to do as the Greeks did?"

"More than that." I felt him press his organ against me.

I licked my lips. "You are placing yourself inside me?"

He laughed. "I love how you phrase it. Yeah, I'm going to fuck you. Hard. And I know you'll be able to take it."

My eyes opened wide as he slowly pressed inside. "Fuck me?" I repeated, dazed, tasting the oft-heard but never-uttered word.

"Don't mind if I do." He pushed further in. It was an... amazing sensation. Alien and yet right. My body accommodated him with hardly a thought from me. Another perk of being made in Heaven rather than on Earth. Then he pushed me upwards into a sitting position and my own weight finished the deed. I gasped as I took his entire length inside me. When I gasped, my wings rose up as well.

"You're gorgeous, angel," he whispered. "Do you know how fucking hot it is to see you sitting on my cock with your pristine feathers all around you?"

"But..." I swallowed, adjusting to the feeling inside me. "But I am still atop you, demon."

He blinked. Then he laughed. Then he began to do as he said he would. He thrust so forcefully that I actually needed my wings out for balance. Knowing that it turned him on, I would have used them to that effect anyway. He held my hands in one of his above his chest.

I could feel him using his feet to gain enough purchase to pump himself inside me. I rose up with each thrust and felt as if I was riding a great beast. In fact, I was. Marbas didn't hold back, pushing into me with great force. It was glorious. I had never truly understood how amazing this could be. Warmth radiated up from where he pierced me, heating as the fever rose up my back and into my wings. They glowed, pulsing with each thrust of him inside me. Marbas groaned as my nearly neon wings lit the apartment in ethereal light. I threw my head back and cried out at his increased vigor. The coffee table beside us vibrated, the floor shaking beneath it.

"The, ah!" I tried to regain my thoughts as I rode him. "The building... it's not strong enough..." I moaned as he pushed up into me hard, my knees came off the ground as he held me up on his hips, his thick thighs taking the weight.

"It'll hold," he growled. "Just a small quake for humans to get in a tizzy about." He pulled me down by his hand around my neck and kissed me hard. His tongue was happily welcomed into my mouth by my own. Something exploded and I could smell ozone burning. When he released me, I could see the remains of the recessed lighting smoking in the ceiling. The owner of the apartment would need to replace all those light bulbs. Before my brain could focus on how many that would be, Marbas quickened his pace, knocking the breath from my lungs.

The glass on the display cabinets began to fog up with steam. One of them cracked from the heat and a spider web of lines raced all over it. It finally sprinkled down in glittery bits revealing its contents which were rattling on their shelves.

I looked down to Marbas who was grinning. He tightened his hands on my own and began to grind into me, swerving his hips instead of thrusting. I gasped and something cracked and fell down onto the floor with a smash. I think it may have been a framed picture. Honestly, this apartment had too much glass for safe sex.

The grinding was amazing. I licked my lips when a thought struck me. "I want..." I panted a few more moments and tried again. "I want... to see... your wings... too," I said between thrusts.

"Yeah?"

"Yes. I... want to see them."

I was tugged down on top of him before being rolled under. He rose up above me in all his demonic glory: his eyes glowed red and his black-skinned wings rose above him.

And I... Well, I came.

Don't judge me.

I cried out, my body convulsing and shivering. My head thrashed and tears sprang to my eyes at the heights of euphoria I achieved. I heard more smashing things and the apartment took on the steamy look of a jungle just after a thunderstorm on a scorching day. When I started to float back down (and having the ability to float, I assure you that is indeed what it feels like), I felt him quicken inside me. He came down on top of me, his hands under my shoulders, holding me to him as he pummeled my body. The floor and walls shook harder, the couch began to vibrate away from us. I reached out and ran a hand along the spine of one of his wings.

And he came.

Now we're even.

He came quietly with only a quickly-indrawn breath, however the gas fireplace in the corner sprang to life with a roar, scorching and blackening the wall above it. The huge TV screen hanging above it began to melt. Marbas' body surged into mine and he held me tightly enough to kill a human. To me, it just felt good.

I drew circles around his nipple. The sound of sirens from emergency vehicles parked in the street below were distant as the flickering of flames danced in the ruined fireplace. We lay on his warm, spread wings while one of mine draped over our entangled legs.

"I should have figured you were a snuggler." I felt, rather than heard, his deep voice under my ear, while my head lay on his chest.

"Of course," I said, with a smile up at him. "I am only giving you what you won."

"We've got plenty of time for that, don't we?"

"Just tonight..." I was stalled by the look in his eye, the smirk on his lips. "It wasn't just tonight?"

"I said the one thing in your power to give. I did not give a time limit."

I looked at him for a moment. I opened my mouth to argue, his eyebrows went up in question, and I closed my mouth. Then I smiled as knowingly as I could (and as a timeless angel, I'm pretty proficient at that).

"Well, you fell right into my plan, demon," I said, as strongly as I could. I was also trying for nonchalant. A strong nonchalantness. "I had heard you were fantastic in the carnal arts and I thought to myself, 'Self, who better to give your chastity away for?' And I was right."

With his eyebrow still raised, he asked in a skeptical tone, "You come up with that just now?"

I kept quiet.

"I think you meant to say that you've been crushing on me for a few decades and always found a way to be around. Your innocent brain wasn't able to figure out that you were hot for me."

I opened my mouth, preparing to argue when he pulled me to him for a kiss.

"Rest up, angel. I'll want my second course shortly."

See? Demons and angels aren't all that different, are they? We both play the Great Game and we do it well. And I am such a magnanimous winner, I wasn't going to tell him that he was right about everything, but one: I knew exactly who I was hot for and what I wanted. He just happened to play right into my hands. But don't fault him. He's just an innocent demon, after all.

If you enjoyed this story, you can sign up for a free membership at
ForbiddenFiction and discuss it with other readers
and the author at the *Devilish Trick* story page
at http://forbiddenfiction.com/library/story/LDD-1.000173

Falling Into Her Arms

Laylah Hunter

Laylah Hunter has been writing erotic fiction for the last decade, starting with fan fiction and branching out into original work when the draw of imagining entire worlds became irresistible. Most of Laylah's work explores speculative themes, queer relationships, power imbalances, or combinations thereof. When not writing, Laylah enjoys long walks through scenic video game landscapes, drinking froofy coffee, and being at the mercy of two very needy cats. It all comes back to the writing eventually, though.

Falling into Her Arms

Time has blurred into a haze of pain and brilliant light; the distant chorus of hymns from the upper reaches of the Tower to Heaven no longer make enough sense to Ambriel's ears for her to mark the passing hours. In her cell the lights are never shut off, a harsh incandescent glare that doesn't end: she is always watched; she can never relax. The thorns twined around her limbs crackle with energy, searing fresh burns as they tighten in response to her smallest movement.

They don't release her until her confessor returns, and by then she's so grateful for the respite that she trembles, the ruins of her wings fluttering behind her and bringing their own fresh bursts of agony.

Grateful enough to tremble, but not enough to speak. Her confessor is a soft-spoken Power with dove gray wings and the gentle mien of a matron, always patient, always asking the same few things: *Tell me where they found you, little sister. Tell me how the Enemy touched you so. Tell me where they hide. You can still come into grace, little sister, but you must repent. Let us into your heart and let this terrible thing end.*

Her heart led her to this cell in the first place; Ambriel says nothing. Her silence is the only gift she can still make to the woman the Tower now seeks. She knows eventually she will break: nobody can withstand the will of Heaven. She has known that since she came into being. (*Nobody?* asks a husky, laughing voice in the back of her mind. *Am I nobody to you?* She remembers the heat of breath against her throat, the teasing trace of fingertips up her thighs.)

There are tears shining in the Power's eyes. "Oh, little sister," she says mournfully. "I hate to see you in such pain. Please. Please, speak to us. Please, let us in." She takes one of Ambriel's hands with an awful gentleness, thumb stroking over the backs of her knuckles.

Once she begins to speak to them, Ambriel doubts she will be able to stop. She can at least hold out a little longer. Perhaps by the time she must confess, her treason will do no harm: the rebels will have moved on, found new routes to travel and new strongholds to defend. Ambriel hopes — but no longer prays — for that much stamina, and keeps her silence.

Her confessor bows over their clasped hands, weeping; her tears sting where they fall on Ambriel's burns. "Oh, child. You could be healed, if you would but speak," the Power says.

Ambriel stirs, biting her tongue. The words that rise to her lips are no confession but an outburst: *Why could I not be healed now?* She clings to that thought, and the answer she knows the Power would never give her: because this is the way of the Tower, to reward only obedience and punish every dissent.

The Power is still speaking, but Ambriel squeezes her eyes shut and does her best not to listen. She thinks of Keteb, of dark tangled hair and a knowing, crooked smile, the heat of a thigh pressed between hers and the smoky sharpness of stolen kisses. She holds to those memories, retreating into them to shut out the unwelcome present. The present fades until her confessor concedes this session and leaves her be.

As the door closes, leaving her alone again, Ambriel's binding thorns spit sparks and hiss back to life. The memories of Keteb dissolve into tatters at the fresh onslaught to her nerves. *Come back*, Ambriel almost cries out — but it would be the confessor who heard her, not Keteb, and she forces the words down.

When the light fails, some vague time after that last session, Ambriel flinches reflexively. The light of the Tower may dim but it never goes *dark*, and now all the electrical systems seem to have failed: the light, the low hum of climate control, the binding thorns, all shut off at once. Distant shouts reach Ambriel from the lower levels, then a low rumble that could be thunder — or an explosion.

Ambriel scrabbles at the thorns, pulling them clumsily away. They prick the soft flesh of her hands but she can't stop, can't let this chance pass by. There's blood on her palms when she fumbles for the manual emergency release on the door, and it takes three tries before she can pry the panel open in the dark. But the release lever still works: the door unseals, letting her out into the wide-open corridor.

The incandescent torches high up on the walls are dark, too, but the crystal windows at the corridor's ends allow a little light to spill inside. Dawn light, Ambriel thinks at first, but no—that's fire, coming up from below. She stumbles to the window and looks. The cut crystal distorts shapes, but the spread of brilliant orange is still clear enough. The district surrounding the Tower to Heaven is burning.

If she takes the flight chambers she'll be found for sure, but there are stairwells for the unfortunate, those who enter the Tower without having the angels' blessing to help them rise to its heights. She could flee, and even if she doesn't win her freedom, she can refuse to be taken alive a second time. New Celestia *needs* the rebels, if this desperation is what the Tower now inspires.

The stairwell is cramped, the space too small and too dark for comfort. Ambriel draws her ruined wings in as best she can, trying to keep the raw edges from brushing the too-close walls. She can smell smoke drifting up from below, and shouts echo off the concrete. The rebels have given up on waiting. *What if she's there?* Ambriel wonders, and pushes the thought away before she can let it paralyze her. All of the rebels have made their choice, and they know the cruelty of angels better than Ambriel does.

She finds the rail by touch, the stairs by slow shuffling steps. The fighting is below and she is high in the tower already; she will climb.

Keteb circles over the streets of Heaven's District, letting the updraft from the flames carry her. The stretched leather and aluminum struts of her wing prostheses creak, but it feels like they're working normally. She's lucky to have kept enough of her own wings to be able to *use* the prostheses in the first place; most of the rebels were more viciously punished, their wings mangled entirely instead of simply pinioned. It's a sign of the Tower's sickness that pinioning is an act of mercy.

As one of the few rebels still capable of flight—assisted or otherwise—Keteb is charged with sabotaging the Tower's attempts to mount an air defense. The main body of the rebel army is advancing on the Tower's ground-level entrances, shields held up in formation to ward off attacks from above. The angels wheel overhead and harry them with light bolts from their lances, focusing more on the grounded army than the few rebels in the air.

Keteb wings one of them with a blast from her lance, feathers scattering and a screech of horror splitting the air as the angel plummets. Already Keteb is turning her attention away, driving herself higher, heading toward the Tower itself. Her shoulders and the remains of her wings ache with effort; all the muscles there have weakened since she lost the ability to fly unaided.

Her target is straight ahead and half a dozen wingbeats higher up: one of the open balconies where the angel warriors launch their attacks. She's carrying a compact, powerful bomb, enough to bring the walls crumbling down and render the launching balcony unusable, one less threat for her sisters and brothers on the ground to face.

The angels manning the balcony see her coming and fire. Keteb rolls, stooping and rising again, answering fire with her lance as their bolts hiss past her. They're shouting as she catches a fortunate thermal and sweeps higher, and she wants to think she hears panic in those voices. The rebels are stronger than they ever imagined.

The thermal gives her enough height. Keteb wheels in toward the Tower, pulling the bomb from her belt and pushing the button to activate it. At the closest point in her arc she throws the bomb, then peels out and away in a dive to get distance from the blast.

It rumbles behind her, and the blast of hot air sends her sprawling, wings beating hard as she fights for stability and altitude. She should have practiced more. Her wings ache, the two parts she still has and phantom pain in the missing third. She turns in the air so she can look back to the Tower: the balcony churns with black smoke, flickering orange flame visible where it thins. Good.

A streak of white against the dark sky catches her attention and Keteb glances left. Someone is falling from the top of the Tower, arms held out helplessly to catch the air, blunted wing-stubs beating to no effect.

Keteb is racing toward the falling angel before she's had time to think. Someone the Tower would treat like that is a friend of the rebels' cause. Wind whistles past Keteb's ears, stinging the corners of her eyes as she stoops into a sharp dive.

She catches the angel a scant two stories above the pavement, jarred by the impact and struggling to stay aloft. The angel makes a soft cry of surprise or pain, clinging to Keteb's harness, and Keteb glances down.

"*Ambriel*?" she gasps. She tries to climb, her muscles burning with the effort of lifting a second body. She's too slow like this, too clumsy to evade another attack. She bears left, sweeping away from the Tower. Not everything in the District is burning.

A few blocks away Keteb comes gliding in for a landing on a flat roof. Her heart is pounding and she's shaking as she sets Ambriel down.

Ambriel looks *terrible*. Her face is too thin, her red hair tangled and unwashed; there are burns twining up her arms and blood smeared on her hands, along with the raw wounds where her wings simply *stop* at the pinion joint. "Oh, mercy," Keteb breathes. "Ambriel, what happened?"

"Keteb," Ambriel whispers. Her eyelids flutter and slowly focus. "You—you came for me?"

"You're safe now," Keteb says, nodding. It's stretching the truth but she doesn't care. Anyone who wants to do Ambriel harm will have to come through her to try it. "I know it must feel terrible, but hold on. We'll help you."

Ambriel nods faintly, her eyes closing again. "I know you will," she says. "They wanted me to tell them about you." She pauses, just breathing, and Keteb's heart aches. "I wouldn't s-say a word."

"Thank you," Keteb says, her voice cracking. She leans down and kisses Ambriel's forehead. "You've been brave and strong. We won't—*I* won't let any more harm come to you."

There is another blur after Ambriel's fall from the Tower, blessed sleep and warm meals blunting the haze of pain. Sometimes she thinks she can hear Keteb's voice, sweet and low, soothing. Her sleep is blissfully dreamless.

The first time she wakes clear-headed, Keteb is there, her form reassuringly familiar: lean limbs and warm brown skin, the tousled fall of her dark hair, the sharpness of her eyes. Even the terribly blunted shapes of her mutilated wings are less unnerving than they once were. There's a scrape on her cheek and a bandage around her arm, but she looks calm, comfortable, *real*. Ambriel smiles.

"You're all right," she says. Her voice comes out hoarse, and Keteb startles at the sound. "I'm glad."

"*I'm* all right?" Keteb says. She shakes her head, reaching out to brush a lock of hair off Ambriel's forehead. "I'm not the one who fell from the Tower after enduring the confessors' persuasion for mercy knows how long."

"I didn't fall," Ambriel says. "I jumped."

Keteb curses in the rebels' cant, a brief explosion of pops and hisses that make a tiny tongue of flame burst from her lips. "Why," she says, when she's gotten control of that outburst. "Why would you—"

"I wasn't trying to die. I didn't realize how helpless they'd left me." Ambriel braces her hands on the mattress and tries to push herself up so she can have this conversation sitting instead of lying on her belly. Her arms tremble, and Keteb reaches to steady her. "I thought—I hoped I could at least glide, with... what I had left."

"If only," Keteb says. She sits next to Ambriel on the edge of the cot. "I'm sorry. Let me start again. How do you feel?"

Ambriel takes a moment to think. "I still ache," she says. "But it's...." She pauses; it's hard to admit. "It's better than I expected to be, after they took me in for confession."

Keteb takes one of Ambriel's hands and lifts it to her lips, kissing each knuckle in turn. The leaders of the Tower claimed that the rebels lost the capacity for kindness, but Ambriel can't believe that anymore.

She leans closer. Keteb releases her hand and meets her for a kiss that tastes like ash. Her lips are soft, her tongue slick and hot. She's ever so gentle, and Ambriel wants to push for more, but she's not sure how much her body can handle right now.

When she pulls back from the kiss, she can see the flickers of heat in Keteb's eyes, golden in the dark. Keteb swallows, visibly relaxing, and says, "We could probably unwrap your arms now, if you want."

Ambriel looks down. She has gauze wrapped from wrist nearly to shoulder on both sides, covering the burns the thorns left. Her legs have been treated likewise. "I think so," she says. "I should—I should see how bad it is." *I should get used to what I've become.*

Keteb kisses her again, then tugs the gauze untucked at one wrist. It unwinds in slow curls, fluttering to the floor. The skin beneath is pale, and the thorns have left scars in twining spirals up the length of Ambriel's arm. They're healed, but barely, still tender, and she's grateful for the softness of Keteb's hands.

"All of them?" Keteb asks.

Ambriel nods. Keteb unwraps her other arm with just as much care. "How did the battle end?" Ambriel asks, as Keteb slips off the cot to kneel at her feet.

"The Tower is fallen," Keteb says. She looks up, Ambriel's heel cradled in her palm. "And Heaven didn't open to scourge us with holy fire after all. The fighting is still going on in the streets, in little skirmishes. But the Tower's authority is broken." The bandages on Ambriel's legs stretch from ankle to knee, and Keteb unwraps them reverently, bending to kiss the new scars.

Ambriel's breath hitches, and she feels a pulse of heat through her clit. "You," she begins, unsure what she wants to say. There is something amazingly illicit about having Keteb kneel to her: forgivable when she had a medical excuse, but achingly taboo when she casts the bandages aside and stays where she is.

"Still thinking about how wrong it is for us to kneel to one another?" Keteb asks, hands on the insides of Ambriel's knees, looking up at her with a knowing smirk. "After experiencing what they think is *right*, I wouldn't think you'd have problems with that anymore."

"I didn't tell you to stop," Ambriel says, and the way Keteb's smile broadens makes her shiver again with anticipation, her nipples stiffening under her thin shift. "What if—what if knowing that it's wrong only makes me want it more?"

Keteb's tongue wets her lower lip, leaves it glistening. "Now you're thinking like a rebel," she says. "Let me see you, beloved. Let me worship you."

Ambriel nods. "I'm in your hands," she says. She reaches for the top ties of her shift, at the nape of her neck, unlacing first those, then the lower pairs beneath her wings. When she shrugs the cloth free of her shoulders, Keteb pulls it away, leaving her bare.

The chill in the air makes her nipples stiffen further, but she thinks even if it were hot as the Pit the way Keteb watches her would be enough. Ambriel spreads her arms, arches her back, offers herself. She has the soft curves of a Tower singer in contrast to Keteb's lean and hungry form: her breasts are ample, her thighs full, the swell of her hips lush.

Keteb slides her hands up Ambriel's thighs, leaning in to kiss a slow path up from her belly to her breastbone before sliding over to take one nipple in her mouth. Ambriel moans at the wet heat and the curl of her tongue, and shivers when Keteb's teeth graze her flesh. "More," she breathes, "more." Keteb hums, bites, runs her nails down Ambriel's thighs and presses her knees further apart.

"So lovely," Keteb murmurs, pulling back to look at her again. Ambriel bites down on the protest—*lovely, after what they've done?*—but it must show in her eyes. "Yes," Keteb says to the question she didn't ask. "Lovely. Strong and brave and unbroken."

Ambriel swallows hard. "You're describing yourself," she says, but the look on Keteb's face is more than just desire. She takes Keteb's hands. "Come up here with me. You're not the only one who wants to touch."

Keteb smiles, letting Ambriel pull her onto the cot. They stretch out on their sides, facing each other, and it takes an awkward, tense moment before Ambriel is sure she can lie like this without harming her wounded wings. But then she has Keteb in her arms, warm and strong, kissing her with the taste of fire still on her lips.

Ambriel catches the rough linen of Keteb's tunic in both hands, holding on tight as their legs twine together. Keteb's thigh slips between hers and presses up hard against the soft folds of her labia; she moans, and tugs Keteb's tunic up so she can return the favor. She can feel slickness there, where Keteb grinds against her, wet heat and the prickle of coarse hair.

Keteb bites her lip, twines needy fingers into her hair, growls low and wild. "Yes," she hisses, her thighs flexing as she pulls Ambriel closer. Her other hand captures the swell of one breast, and she rolls Ambriel's nipple between her fingers. Pleasure blazes along Ambriel's nerves and her hips buck; Keteb croons an incoherent, fiery string of endearments in the rebels' cant that makes Ambriel grind up harder against her.

The rough pressure makes Keteb's hands falter—her head falls back and she moans, her wings flexing and trembling behind her, little stuttering motions as if she could still take flight. Her breathing is harsh, shaky, and Ambriel finds her own body humming with tension as she watches, pushes—she bites at Keteb's throat and Keteb sobs, shuddering against her, slicking Ambriel's thigh with the fluids of her climax.

She barely takes a breath to recover before she's kissing Ambriel hard, careless teeth and rough tongue. Her fingers snarl in Ambriel's hair and drag her head back so she can bite, hungry and sensual, as her other hand slides down to press between Ambriel's legs.

Ambriel bucks into her hand as Keteb's fingers part her folds and find her soaking wet, shuddering at every glancing touch to her clit, whimpering with need as Keteb's fingertips circle the opening of her cunt. "Please," she gasps, "ah—Keteb, *please.*"

Keteb's fingers slip into her and she arches her back, pushing down to meet them and take them deep. The heel of Keteb's hand comes to rest against the hood of her clit and Ambriel moans. The rest of the world dims, fades away and leaves only this moment, these sensations, the thrust of Keteb's fingers and the rocking motion of her hand, the friction and heat. Ambriel pushes into each thrust, driving herself harder onto Keteb's hand. Each stroke brings a new jolt of pleasure through her nerves, and she tries to coax Keteb into giving her *more*, but Keteb refuses to be hurried—she keeps her pace, steady as beating wings, her fingers crooked forward to rub the tender spot there. Ambriel feels molten, reduced to a thrum of liquid heat and need, caught by Keteb's merciless, clever fingers and trembling ever closer to the edge. Her breath hitches and for an instant the tension is too much to bear, before climax wracks her, leaves her shaking and gasping and soaking wet.

And oh, Keteb looks pleased with herself. She eases her hand free gently and raises it to her lips, licking her fingers clean. Ambriel laughs breathlessly. "You are so—"

"Incorrigible?" Keteb asks with a grin.

"Wonderful," Ambriel answers. She doesn't have to leave, she realizes. They don't have to part ways. She isn't going back to the Tower ever again; she can stay with Keteb and they can learn to share their lives, instead of only the moments they can steal.

This particular moment doesn't need to be over, either. The thought is energizing, *thrilling*. Ambriel disentangles herself enough to rise up on her knees and slide further down the cot. There's a brief warning throb from her right wing, but she settles them close against her back and the pain subsides.

Keteb sits up, raising an eyebrow. "You seem to be recovering quickly," she says.

"I've been well cared for," Ambriel smiles. She presses Keteb's thighs apart and Keteb leans back on her hands, knees raised and heels braced to the edges of the cot. Her cunt glistens, wet and deep pink, and Ambriel can smell her musk. "I think it would be only fair for me to return the favor."

She lowers herself carefully between Keteb's thighs and leans in to taste, savoring the rich salt, delighting in the knowledge that she can stay, that she can take her time and enjoy this. "Yes," Keteb moans, one hand finding hers and clutching tight. Ambriel laces their fingers together as she parts Keteb's folds with her tongue.

The Tower may be lost, but Ambriel has finally found her way home.

If you enjoyed this story, you can sign up for a free membership at
ForbiddenFiction and discuss it with other readers
and the author at the *Falling into Her Arms* story page
at http://forbiddenfiction.com/library/story/LH2-1.000143

Icarus Bleeds

Annabeth Leong

Annabeth Leong found relief in erotica. Reading others' stories opened up a world of freedom and exploration. Writing it increased the thrill. Since her first published story in 2009, she has written for anthologies by Cleis Press, Ravenous Romance, Coming Together, and Circlet. Her work has appeared online at Every Night Erotica and Oysters and Chocolate. She is pleased to participate in Forbidden Fiction's Special Collections. Besides freedom of speech, Annabeth loves shoes, stockings, cooking, and attending concerts—probably in that order. She lives in Providence, Rhode Island.

Chapter 1

A Dream of Wings

I will call him Icarus, because he worked so hard to erase his birth name that I will not commit the sin of returning it to him now. The things I said and did when I knew him will only make sense if you understand how beautiful he was, so I will try to force the words of mortals to describe a man who never seemed to belong to earth at all.

Icarus first came to me in the dark, in the rain, passing out of the shadows falling over the street, slipping smoothly into the shadows I made for myself. His eyes glowed from the corner where he took a seat, huddled under shelves loaded with discarded computer equipment. Even then I wondered how a shadow could be so luminous within a shadow, how black could shimmer from within black.

I wasn't in the habit of looking at my clients. They came because they wanted to be forgotten, and they generally did not want to be seen either. I could not help myself with Icarus. He reminded me of flesh I liked to pretend I didn't have. Eyes, lips, fingertips, inner thighs, the sides of my stomach, the soles of my feet. And, yes. Tongue. Cock. Thoughts both crude and poetic competed to distract me from the mechanical process of obscuring someone from all the files and IP addresses that affirmed that person's existence.

I avoided looking at his skin, a lighter shade of what is called black than my own purple-tinged pigment. Icarus's brand of black flowed with honey, shone with sunlight, glittered with the gold that may once have belonged to Pharaoh. Long, thin fingers, delicate as a girl's. Red-gold palms, and the beginnings of a scar, a telltale revelation of a story that started in the hands and parted the flesh of the forearm nearly to the elbow.

He saw me looking, and pulled the sleeves of his sweater down low, clutching bunches of the material in clenched fists. "Can you really make me disappear?"

I snorted. "Of course not. Not these days, not with the backups they keep and the triple cross checks they have to avoid failure conditions. Best I can do is make them forget to look for you."

He nodded, the gesture emphasizing the length of his neck, the quality of his silence. "How much?"

"How much you got?"

He shrank back from me, receding into the forest of parts and cords. "I'm not looking for favors."

"I don't do favors. I do a sliding scale. You pay what you can afford to pay. What you think is fair. I trust you."

"Why?"

I sighed. No one ever understood this when I bothered to explain. "Because I'm not one of them. I don't want to act like one."

He swallowed, his Adam's apple moving gracefully up and down in that impossibly lean neck. "I was going to see what you would take." He bit his lip and didn't explicate, but I got an idea of what he'd had in mind by the way his hands crept toward his fly, the gesture so subtle that I wasn't sure it had been a conscious invitation.

On any other night, with any other man, I wouldn't have. I would have kissed that smooth, wide forehead, done my work for free, and sent him back into the street uttering the vague promise that someday, when he could, he would take care of me. With Icarus, I could not resist the offer. I had to keep him a little longer. Though I hated myself for it, the sentence passed my lips as if it made up part of my daily stock in trade. "After I finish, you'll come upstairs with me."

His bowed head telegraphed his acquiescence well before his soft words. "Thank you."

When I got him to my bed, I knew I should be the one thanking him. He stripped with a benevolent dignity that shamed me. I felt as if I'd brought the Virgin Mary to my room to make a whore of her. Again, I considered releasing him, leaving my work to be my offering to his present and future beauty.

Then his undershirt peeled away from smooth, hard abs, and his boxers fell away from his hips and the thick, dark cock that hung soft between his legs. The shy and lovely youth before me, with his incandescent eyes and visible ribs, brought my own cock surging to life. I could not let him go. My desire made me cruel.

"Get on your knees and crawl to me," I whispered, loosening my own clothing, casting it aside. Hurt flashed through his eyes, and

I loved it for the confirmation that it offered. He was open to me. I could touch him. I could make him remember me forever.

His lean, taut muscles rippled. Icarus could not move without grace. He glorified my floor by lowering himself to it. His knees and palms left a trail through the dust of my unswept room as he crossed to me.

I lifted my right foot. He did not need to be told. Icarus lowered himself onto his elbows and pressed a kiss to the arch of my foot. I shivered. The surface of his lips scratched coarsely against my foot, but the soft, hot padding beneath soothed me utterly. His kisses continued up my sole, methodically, their heat lingering everywhere they touched.

"Suck," I said, hissing with pleasure when he took my largest toe in his mouth, then stuffed in smaller toes beside it. I gritted my teeth to avoid kicking him, the warm, wet pleasure of his inner cheek unbearable when combined with the light scrape of his teeth and the rough caress of his tongue. He shifted position and lifted one hand to support my foot. I could not remember a man's hands ever being so smooth, so entirely free of calluses, and yet so strong. He pumped my foot in and out of his mouth, as much of it as he could fit inside, his lips stretching obscenely to accommodate me.

Icarus kissed and licked my calluses, nibbled on them lightly, and opened his mouth and ran his lower set of teeth with exquisite care over my instep and up toward my ankle. His cock had hardened, and my own cock threatened to burst at the sight of his total concentration, and the earnestness with which he sucked on what he'd been given to suck.

"The other one." He moaned and switched. I set my damp right foot on the floor, where it cooled from the fire of his mouth. Bracing one hand against the wall behind me, I fed him the left foot, faster this time, wriggling my toes inside his mouth, wanting him to struggle to take me in.

Icarus gave himself to me, holding the foot with both hands, writhing on the floor below me, eyes closed, mouth and throat open to an alarming degree.

I should have played with him longer, but again I could not. I pulled my foot out of his grasp, leaned over, and gripped him under the armpits, hauling him up and into my kiss. I felt so clumsy compared to him, my hands desperate and fumbling to feel his ass, the subtle muscles of his back, the outsides of his legs. His cock settled against mine, velvet heat to velvet heat. He sighed as he gave his mouth to me, and all I wanted was to push in deeper.

"Get on the bed." My words barely more than a breath. I had no right to this, and yet I would go on taking it until forced to stop. I tore through drawers until I found a mostly full bottle of lube, untouched aside from my infrequent bouts of self-abuse. Unbelievably, I still had rubbers, not even expired.

I flung myself onto Icarus's body, kissing the back of his neck, stroking his sides, smelling the oil in his hair, biting his shoulders a few times. My fingers found his cock and closed around it, but I sought my pleasure, not his, so I did not stroke him. I just held it, enjoying the warmth that radiated from the hard length and into my palm. I reached around him with the other hand and cupped his balls, squeezing them gently so I could relish their vulnerability.

Breath and blood moved through his body as it rested within my embrace. Releasing his cock, I pressed my hand lightly to his throat. He trembled. My balls ached. I kissed the spot beside my hand, then slid down in one firm stroke, gripping the curve of his ass. Firm, ripe muscle filled my hand. Seeking deeper, my fingers parted the cheeks, caressed the valley between them, found his hole.

He jerked when I touched it. He was no hardened whore. "Have you done this before?" I whispered.

"No," he said. It might have been a lie, but it was what I wanted to hear. I petted his head, murmured in his ear, and teased and caressed that hole, its ring of muscle jumping in response to my every movement.

I collected lube on my fingers and rubbed it into him, swirling around his hole, beginning to push the barest bit inside. His body was so hot, its grip so tight, that I wanted to come just imagining what his ass would feel like around my cock.

"Are you scared?"

"No."

"Open up for me."

I pressed one finger in, and his body went stiff in my grip. He drew a shaking breath and writhed to get away, suddenly fighting me where before there had been only acquiescence. My hand froze, then eased out of him. He lay gasping in my arms.

"OK, maybe I am scared."

I managed some compassion for the first time in a while. "Do you want to stop?"

He stayed silent for so long that I was tempted to take the lack of words as tacit permission and start playing with his ass again. I forced myself to wait, clenching my fingers to keep them still.

"No," he said finally, though I had to strain to hear him. "I want you."

"You do?" I could not keep the shock out of my voice. In response, he only nodded, keeping his face turned away. "Why?"

He shrugged, pulled my hand back toward his ass. I wanted to roll him onto his belly and just fuck him. Hard, triumphant victory filled my chest. But his expression of desire had destroyed my appetite for cruelty. I rubbed his back as my finger resumed teasing his hole, as gently and sweetly as I could. "Tell me about a beautiful thing," I said. "Something that you think about that might help you relax."

"Wings." I felt his smile where his face pressed against my chest, but also in the sigh that passed over his body along with the word, leaving Icarus transformed in its wake.

"The wings of birds? Airplanes?" His ass had changed so much that it was almost sucking my finger in. I wanted to keep him talking.

"The wings of men," Icarus sighed. "In the Central City, within the walls, you see them flying all hours of day and night. You know they're not angels, but they look like they are. That's not even the point, though. They go so high. It looks like almost to the sun. And it's got to all look so different up there. You've got to feel free."

I'd gotten two fingers into his ass by then, and had my other hand stroking his cock and balls. He shuddered with pleasure now as I worked my fingers in and out of him and dropped kisses along his neck and shoulder blade. I got a little distracted trying to place his accent. He had the flat, universal sound most of us have picked up from the Internet, but something changed when he mentioned Central City. I didn't think there were any black people in the upper echelon. As a courtesy, I never looked into my clients' histories while I obscured them, but now I wondered who he was.

A little whimper brought me back to more pressing concerns, and the need to help him stay inside his fantasy. "You ever seen one of those angel-men on the ground?"

A nod. "I used to climb up to the top of the Skywalk. They like to land up there. The view is nice, and there's a good restaurant. That restaurant has towels for them, to wipe off the condensation they pick up from flying through the clouds."

I grunted. "To wipe off sweat, more likely."

"No!" The innocent wonder in his voice made me feel old. "Their faces have little frost crystals on them. Their wings are pale because the blood shrinks back in the skin under the feathers when it gets cold. When they warm up again, the wings get a rosy glow from the blood returning."

"You know a lot about this." I slid a third finger into him. At this rate, he'd be ready for my cock sooner than I could have hoped.

"The operation is too expensive."

"It doesn't have to be." I shouldn't have said that, but my pulsing cock had destroyed my thinking by then. I needed inside him, and those words seemed like my golden key. I twisted my fingers, stroking the inner walls of his ass, while I pumped his cock with my other hand. Icarus moaned and pressed back toward me.

"What do you mean?"

"Nothing is impossible, kid. Outside of Central City, we learn to take what we want."

"You really think so?"

"Hell, yes, I think so."

He closed his eyes, obviously caught in his dream of flight. His whole body softened, except for his cock, which had gotten so hard it was quivering. I put on the rubber, lubed up my cock, and took a chance, lining up the head and holding my breath as I eased my way in.

Icarus made a little sound in the back of his throat. "You think I could—"

"Get wings yourself. Yeah." I spoke between gritted teeth, probing ever deeper with my cock. "I can just see how pretty those wings would look on you, spread out to either side of your hot little body, feathers brushing this round ass of yours, your muscles rippling while you pump those wings up and down."

I was fully fucking him by then, gaining confidence in the power of these magical words I had discovered. His ass welcomed my every stroke. Beneath me, he whimpered and arched his back, taking me in to the hilt. "Yes," he whispered. I wasn't sure if he approved of my cock or my words, but I didn't really care.

I grabbed his shoulders. "You could fly up past the buildings. Up even higher than the clouds." I fucked him so hard my words came out as gasps. "Big, wide wings. Tall wings. Whatever color feathers you want."

His ass, for all of its compliance, massaged my cock with such a tight and persistent grip that every inch I sank into Icarus sent nerves tingling down to my feet and up to my head. I was seconds from orgasm, babbling incoherently by then, spewing out whatever wing-related words I could think of. A man will say some stupid things when his cock is happy, especially when it hasn't been for a long time.

"You find somewhere to get wings," I panted. "I'll take you there and help you check them out. Hell, I could even pay for it."

"You would do that?" His cock jumped in my hand. I pumped it faster.

"Yes," I said. His ass clenched around me. My cock had never felt that good before. I pushed in as deep as I could and ground my hips in a circle. Icarus came, pumping his seed out onto my fingers. I felt his balls, drawn up tight and wrinkled near where I gripped the base of his cock.

Icarus reached behind himself for me, face a portrait of ecstasy, and pulled me even deeper into his spasming ass. I growled and fucked myself the rest of the way toward heaven. Who needed wings to fly when I had him?

Only later, holding him in the darkness, did I think about what I'd promised him. I could tell the wings were serious for him. If he trusted me, if he thought I might really give them to him, maybe he would stay. I closed my eyes, clasping the slick, soft heat of Icarus's sweat-soaked back tightly against my chest. I wanted him to stay.

Chapter 2
Wings of Blood and Wax

We talked all the time about how hot it would be for Icarus to have wings, and how beautiful they would look. Wings were foreplay, but they were also hope, joy, and the proof that I wasn't just a horny old bastard taking advantage of a man half my age. I had something good to offer, and Icarus could have it as soon as he found a shop that could do it.

He lived at my place, soft and warm beside me every morning, the light layer of fuzz on his skin already seeming feathery when I rolled toward him for the day's first kiss. I tried not to question it. I didn't want to encourage any line of discussion that might make him realize how much better he could do for himself.

We didn't talk about how expensive wings were, and what I would have to do to actually set him up with them. I stayed up once calculating it. My usual finance policies didn't lead to huge savings. I'd always liked it that way, partly because I could think of myself as a good guy, and partly because it helped me fly under the radar. I would have to behave differently if I wanted to pay for wings for Icarus. I would have to take riskier jobs, for people I liked less.

I saved the calculations in an encrypted file and crept upstairs to bed. Icarus sighed at my touch, snuggling into me, and I couldn't help suckling his cock until he woke up and let me fuck him. I could pretend I had a choice about this, but the truth spooned with me every night in my bedroom. When the time came to come up with the money, I knew I had to deliver. I could never bear to see my image darken in Icarus's luminous black eyes. I could not disappoint him.

"I scheduled the operation for Wednesday," Icarus whispered. I held him a minute before I spoke.

I'd been to check out the shop after he found it, and I hadn't liked the guy in charge. His hands seemed too rough, too clumsy, too uncaring. I didn't like his big-breasted tattoo. I didn't like the idea of him touching Icarus at all, ever. "Can't you look for somewhere else?"

He went stiff and ashen, and pulled back from me. "There's nowhere else, OK? Not outside Central City! Believe me, I've looked everywhere. This guy says he's got state of the art equipment."

"That's what he *says*."

"You don't understand. You don't need this. You don't need anything. You're happy with what you've got right now. You want me to wait so I still need you."

My face must have betrayed me, because Icarus smiled horribly. He turned his back and stripped, then leaned over and spread his ass cheeks—not with his usual innocent sensuality, but lewdly. "Put your clothes back on," I told him.

"What's the matter? I thought this was what you wanted. Don't you get enough of it? Don't you get to fuck me whenever you want?" His voice rose hysterically.

It might have been better to keep my hands off him, but again I could not. I scooped him into my arms, tugged his boxers back up his hips myself, pulled him over to the bed. I clasped him against my chest, rubbing his back, ashamed of my growing erection. "That's not what this is," I said, desperate to soothe him. But my own fears emerged against my will, turning my voice petulant. "I didn't want to force you. You said you wanted me."

"I said what you wanted to hear."

Pain hissed through my chest. I thrust him away from me and jumped up from the bed. I knew better than to think someone like Icarus would really choose me, for my own merits, but I must have let myself slip into the fantasy his ongoing presence inspired.

Regret flashed through his eyes. "Hey. I'm sorry. I didn't mean it."

"Of course you didn't." I kept my back to him. Tears welled up in my eyes, threatening to fall. I couldn't let him see them.

"I'm sorry."

"I know." I sighed. "I'm worried about you, but it's your decision. If you want this guy to do your operation, I'll take you there on Wednesday."

His arms wrapping around my hips could already have been the wings of grace. I even smiled as he pulled me back to bed. He had never been so enthusiastic with me before—his mouth engulfing my cock, hands cupping my balls, legs intertwined with mine—but I could not let myself sink into the sensation of him. He tried to talk me off by going on about the wings, but that wasn't working for me just then. Icarus could tell, and I had to wipe that disappointed look off his face before it broke my heart.

I flipped him onto his stomach and felt up his shoulder blades. I couldn't stop picturing that chop man slicing them up, and my cock wilted completely. I moaned anyway, trying to pretend the whole thing turned me on. I didn't want to think about him scarred. I didn't want to think about him changed.

He was perfect the way he was, but what he'd said about me had been the truth, too. I couldn't understand. As long as I had him, I didn't need anything. He had all of me, everything I could give, but that didn't do fuck-all toward giving him anything he actually needed or even wanted.

Icarus glanced behind him. I'd forgotten to keep up my moaning. I smiled and stroked a finger down his cheek. My perfect boy. Tonight, he was mine, bare and glowing and completely natural. I reached between his legs and stroked behind his balls, and the sweetness of his responding cry got my cock interested again. I spread his cheeks and buried my face in his ass, kissing him, tasting him. I'd never wanted to do things like that before, but there wasn't anything about Icarus that I didn't want to touch or smell or put in my mouth or rub with my fingers or the bottoms of my feet or any part of me that he would allow.

I lubed his ass and tried to fuck him, but he started muttering about wings again. I cursed myself for encouraging that habit.

Eventually, I gave up on coming. I faked my groans of pleasure, wiggled my cock like it was spurting, and jerked him off hard. Then

I lay awake and clutched him so tightly he complained he couldn't sleep.

I liked to fly under the radar. I helped people nobody cared about, people the authorities behind the Central City databases wouldn't mind forgetting. I made sure those people knew how to find me, and nobody else.

See, the systems are more powerful than anybody needs. The computer will flag anybody who breaks any rule, and it's not designed to determine how significant that rule or that person is. Once you get tagged that way, you're make-work for the enforcers. You're effectively a walking pile of paperwork they have to do, an inflated selection of an overwhelming to-do list. For them, it makes more sense to shoot you than to take you in—that's one page of paperwork, versus reams of it.

My usual procedure turned out to help everyone. I made the enforcers happy because I could take you out of the system. A pile of paperwork becomes no paperwork at all—not even the one page that a bullet requires. You were happy because I could sanitize the ID chips behind your retinas, which meant you could go pay cash in the corner store without getting shot by a lazy enforcer. I was happy because I could get by on your gratitude and any scraps you saw fit to throw me.

That was how it used to work. For Icarus, I needed more.

The morning after he told me about his appointment, I worked up a new ID for myself. I posted it on the sites I used to avoid, where people who've actually done something look for someone desperate and good enough to make them disappear.

I knew how to sweep up the refuse that piled up in the corners of the system, but this new work required prying Central City's grip loose from people it still wanted to control. I called myself Daedalus, and my guts twisted as the offers poured in.

"Stay in the room and watch? Are you crazy? I'd have to tie you down and gag you to make sure you didn't do anything to distract me."

"If that's what you have to do," I said. Icarus rolled his eyes as if I were an overprotective parent, but I told myself he would be relieved, too, once it was happening.

The chop shop seemed all too worthy of its name. Through a large window, I saw a room with surgical tools and an operating table—though not the kind you'd find in a hospital. Handcuffs fitted at both ends suggested it doubled as dungeon equipment, or possibly something less pleasurable for the party attached to the table. The room we occupied could have been a machine shop. Rusty gears and rustier circular saws competed for space with outdated cash registers, overturned work tables, radar detectors, and who knew what else. A layer of sawdust coated the floor, and I couldn't vouch for how clean the medical room would be.

I hadn't been able to keep my breakfast down. I wasn't losing this battle. I didn't care what I had to do.

The owner of the chop shop sank deeper into his sales pitch. "I'll give him your money's worth, old man. You don't have to worry about getting cheated. Real titanium-structured wings, feathers harvested from swans and eagles, everything totally legit. Nanocyte healing gels, the works."

"I watch, or it doesn't happen."

The man scowled. "Grab a lollipop and a seat, sweetheart," he said to Icarus. He took me by the arm and pulled me into a side room, this one crammed full of packing material. I wrinkled my nose at the sour smell of his skin. I wondered about his general hygiene, and made a mental note to insist he wear latex gloves, too.

The chop man hawked a little into the back of his throat and squinted at me. "I get it, man. If I was Daddy to that sweet little piece of meat out there, I'd never want to take my eyes off him either. But I'm not going to grab his cock while I'm working on him. He's all yours. He'll be great advertising for me, looking the way he does and wearing my wings. I'm going to do this right."

"I gave you my conditions."

Now, the conspiratorial smile. The pat on the outside of my arm to show that we were both friends, that we were more alike than different. I folded my arms against my chest and cocked my head to hear the next phase of his pitch.

"Why do you want to see this, Daddy? He's going to bleed. He's going to get hurt. You don't want to watch me drilling holes in his scapulas. Do you?"

Of course I didn't. Just the thought of that made me dizzy. But it wasn't as bad as the idea of catching a glimpse through the curtain he would draw over that big window, or of pacing outside over that sawdust-covered floor, wondering about every buzzing sound I heard. I shook my head slightly.

"Have it your way," the chop man growled. "But I wasn't kidding about restraining you. You know that, right?"

"Oh, you're damn right. If you don't tie me down, I'll fucking kill you the moment you touch his skin with your knife."

"Wonderful. We'll call it a deal."

Icarus bled. I bled from my eyes in sympathy, thick drops falling down my cheeks to match the drops that fell from his would-be wings to stain the thick layer of sawdust in the makeshift operating room. When they trickled into the corners of my mouth, they tasted only of salt, only of my sweat and effort, but even if they didn't contain the iron produced in my heart, I know I must have bled.

The chop man drugged him heavily, coaxing needle after needle into the pristine veins of his left arm, then more into the areas around his shoulder blades, but he didn't put Icarus all the way under. I had to listen to his gasps of surprise, odd little moans, and occasional slurring giggles.

It was hell. So much adrenaline pumped through my veins that I worried the man hadn't tied me tight enough. I thought the slightest motion would burst the bonds that held me.

Icarus came apart before my eyes. The chop man opened him, made his shoulders weep fluid down the curve of his back, past his ass. The pinkish mess drooled down his upper thighs and into the backs of his knees. Flesh tore. Bone protested. The chop man drilled and hacked, pinned and sutured. Feathers soaked in pools of wax, waiting to be sealed and inserted.

Bound to the table, Icarus made swooshing noises like a little boy playing with an action hero. He flinched when the chop man fitted titanium rods into his perforated shoulder blades, but then his sighed like an even younger child. "Wings."

"Yeah, buddy. Wings." The chop man shot me a look for the outburst and snapped another rod into place.

The structure dwarfed Icarus, the wings looming over him like a twisted metal angel. "How's he going to move all that?" I asked.

"Questions weren't part of the deal," the chop man said. "I know what I'm doing. He's going to look real pretty."

"Is he going to be able to fly?"

The chop man paused too long. "Sure. Of course. Once he heals."

"He says the wings in Central City let people fly."

"This isn't Central City."

I glared at the chop man's back, focusing on the spot where sweat soaked his grimy T-shirt. "Don't I know it."

That was the moment I knew I was right to despair. The chop man worked for five more hours on wings for Icarus, but I couldn't lift my eyes to look at them anymore. I watched the blood and wax that dripped off the operating table and into the sawdust. The byproducts. The refuse that would never quite be swept away. The things that would stain.

Chapter 3
The Agony of Flight

Icarus required a complex geometric process to get through any door at my place. That didn't matter too much, because he mostly had to stay in bed, gasping and sweating and oozing blood from the holes in his shoulder blades. Most of the feathers on his wings had turned pink from all the mess.

Bed presented its own problems. Icarus could not lie on his swollen back, of course. I could not lie beside him. Even if I'd been able to stand the smell of his infected flesh, I couldn't have gotten close enough to hold him.

Lying on his stomach wasn't comfortable either. To do that without suffocating, Icarus had to twist his head to one side, which engaged the muscles in his neck, which were attached to the screwed-up muscles in his shoulder blades.

Turns out you use the muscles in your shoulder blades a lot. Anytime you want to turn your torso or lift your head or move your arms at all. I tried to find a way to make him comfortable, but his wings prohibited him from sitting in any chair, and when he tried to stand he could not walk more than a few feet without jostling the painful mass of titanium and feathers.

I slept downstairs in my work room. I'd been busy anyway, dealing with the clients I'd had to take on to make the necessary payments to the chop man. Sometimes, through the ceiling, I could hear him crying. Worse, I sometimes heard his moans of agony as he tried to flap his new set of wings.

"You need to eat," I told him one morning. "You can't heal if all you do is drink water."

The eyes that returned my concerned gaze chilled me. Black, dead, and hopeless, they remained empty of both reproach and sign of life. I had to look away from the body I once worshiped.

Oatmeal, sweetened with a little honey. A bowl I hadn't used in a long time, dug out so I could hold it without memories of another, happier Icarus. A spoon, gleaming and fitted to its proper use. I held this up to swollen lips, which responded only slightly. "Please," I said. "Eat for me, if not for you."

His sudden laugh knocked the oatmeal off the spoon and the spoon out of my hand and onto the floor. I bent to retrieve it, trying to clean it with the corner of my shirt, one eye peering up to read his face.

"I still need you," Icarus whispered, his voice cracking from illness and disuse. "I thought these wings would make me free, but now I can never, never leave. You must think it's funny."

Again, the stab of pain. I'd been selfish in my desire for his body, but I'd never wanted to force him, to make him feel trapped. "If there's anywhere else you want to go," I offered, swallowing my fear and loss. "I'll do whatever it takes to get you where you need to be."

For answer, Icarus nudged the bowl out of my hand, hissing with pain at the slight movement of his arm. We both ignored the oatmeal spilling onto the floor. "I'm where I need to be," he said. "I'm where I want to be."

He pulled me close against him, creating an embrace inch by agonizing inch. His arms shook from the strain of reaching around me. His breath caught in his throat. His heart pounded so hard I felt it in my own breastbone. His stomach quivered. I knew better than to fight him or offer to help, and finally, I stood as gently as I could, a little of his blood soaking into the clothes I wore.

My cock proved blind to the tragedy of the moment, hardening in its usual response to Icarus. I winced an apology, but my would-be angel only smiled. "You love me, don't you?" he said. "For real. Like it hurts."

I should have said it back, out loud, but I only ducked my head and nodded, feeling like a pathetic old man. I moved to kiss his chin, and he caught my mouth with his lips. I moaned, startled and excited. I forgot the smell of sickness and remembered all the nights we had been together in that room. I should have given him more pleasure on the first night. I resolved to make it up to him.

Tip of the tongue down his throat, fingers flicking lightly over his chest, watching the muscles twitch in response to my touch. Icarus was always thin, but that time I could taste his ribs through his skin. Fear of disturbing his costly embrace kept me in place for a long time, loving him as best I could with only the edges of myself, and trying not to move him at all.

His cock moved, lengthening and requiring me to carefully adjust to make room for it to rise. I held my breath as I used my lower body to maneuver it into place between our stomachs. My own cock had long ago lost interest, fallen victim to the crimes of concentration and concern.

The heat of Icarus's cock penetrated my clothes. I shifted cautiously so I could slide one hand down to wrap around it. I stroked him awkwardly from the bad angle, until Icarus sobbed from the back of his throat and said, "Please. I need to feel your mouth."

He loosened his arms from around me and let them fall bonelessly to his sides, grunting. I sank to my knees before him. Tilting my head back, I met his eyes. He watched so remotely that I saw him as a broken, bloodied angel in truth. I parted my lips and took his cock like penance.

Little mewls of pleasure from above were interrupted by the occasional click of the tongue or hiss when I jarred his body too strongly. I forced myself to keep my pace slow and gentle, pulling his cock all of the way out of my mouth each time and then letting my lips push his foreskin back as I eased it back inside.

He filled my mouth as much as ever, but the pleasure I gave him seemed far too weak. I flicked my tongue over the head of his cock as it passed on its journey to the depths of my throat. I tried sucking until my cheeks hollowed. I aborted my attempt at deep-throating when it became clear that he couldn't stay standing under the pressure of me pushing his cock through the resistance at the back of my mouth. It made me feel so useless.

I would have caressed him, but I feared hurting that way, too. My hands remained at my sides. My knees began to ache from holding my weight on the wooden floor. Still, I licked him, and fucked him slowly with my mouth.

Icarus made the effort of lifting a hand again so it could rest on the top of my head. His groans as his hand moved back and forth with my bobbing head eventually became too much for me. Releasing his cock, I touched a fingertip to his wrist as lightly as I could. "Doesn't it hurt you?"

Icarus twitched his cock in answer. Remarkably, it hadn't gone soft. "I'm thinking about how you gave me my wings."

The only thing that prevented me from falling back in horror was worry about what that would do to the hand on my head. "That's still a good thing?"

"When I get better," Icarus said, "I'm going to fly." With that, he grabbed the back of my head and pushed his cock deep into me, screaming as he did. I didn't know if it was pain or pleasure, but I wasn't about to refuse him. I sucked him hard and fast, taking his actions as permission to ignore the possibility of causing him pain.

An eternity passed. My jaw ached. The back of my throat burned. I'd sucked saliva up my nose trying to breathe around his cock. I couldn't have gotten off my knees if I wanted to.

Slowly, Icarus's ass began to move, to pump his cock into me. I groaned. I'd gotten hard again. I let one hand make its way down to my own cock as I increased my pace on his. I took myself in my fist and thought of his sweet ass, of the things I hoped to do to him again one day.

I'd learned by then to ignore the harsh breathing above me and the occasional sobs. I just followed the command of Icarus's hand, which still jerked occasionally in my hair. For a moment, I forgot the operation. I smelled Icarus's skin, and anticipated the moment he would come in my mouth.

His cock began to spurt, and my hand moved more vigorously. Victory surged down my spine and into my cock as Icarus came for me.

But my hard-on wilted suddenly as he uttered a little bleat and fell backwards, his terrible, delicate wings crashing into the wall behind him. The cry that followed tore at me.

I tried to scramble to my feet, but my legs had fallen utterly asleep during my long bout of cocksucking. I flailed helplessly on the floor, struggling to master my leaden limbs, while Icarus stood in silent agony, biting a trembling lip and gripping his naked thighs with hands like claws.

"Are you OK?"

He did not respond. Agonizingly long moments later, I finally managed to stand, to go to him.

"The wings?"

I examined his back. Fresh blood flowed from his wounds, but the titanium rods held true. Much as I wanted to murder the chop man, I could not question the strength of the attachments he had fitted onto Icarus. "They're in place," I told him.

To my amazement, a beatific smile eclipsed the pain on Icarus's face. "Thank you," he said.

"For what?"

"For making me come."

"You fell."

"I needed it."

I didn't want to contradict him. I kissed his cheek. Part of me savored the salty-sour semen taste that lingered along the sides of my tongue and toward the back of my throat, but to another part of me, it tasted like guilt.

"I want to do you," Icarus whispered.

"How?" I couldn't have asked it of him even if I thought it was possible.

"Get on a chair. Stand on it. I can't kneel, but if you can get yourself high enough, I can probably dip."

"I can't let you—"

"Please." The naked need in his voice far surpassed the way he'd sounded asking me to suck him. I could not refuse. I went downstairs for my desk chair, hauling it up the awkward, curving stairs and into the cramped bedroom without a thought about how I would get it down again.

I stripped and climbed onto the chair. Icarus's face twisted as he struggled to get into a position where he could reach my cock. He tried bracing his hands against my legs, but his arms began to shake and he eventually pulled back with a gasp. He cycled through a number of difficult-looking positions until he ended up sharing the seat of the chair with me, one knee on either side of my feet. The height of the chair allowed him to kneel without having to press the bottoms of his wings into the floor.

From there, Icarus strained and grunted until he managed to get his face into my crotch. By then, all arousal had left me long before. I felt like a heartless bastard.

"Sorry," I muttered. "Give me a minute."

I closed my eyes and remembered the nights I'd held him spooned against my chest, no wings in the way, and no pain. My hard cock would wake me up at night more often than not, and I would try to pull slightly back from Icarus and jerk myself off without waking him. The times I wasn't quiet or subtle enough, he'd wake, sigh slightly, and slip under the covers to offer me his mouth. The familiar sense of selfishness would burn in the pit of my stomach, but I wouldn't protest. I would stroke his hair, tug lightly on his ears, trace the shape of his lips stretched around my cock.

That soft, hot mouth closed around my cock now. I grunted with lust, even as he whimpered with pain. The erection I had managed slipped. I opened my eyes and looked down. Blood oozed down his wings. His body trembled from holding himself in position. The lines around his eyes spoke of effort and discomfort.

For a moment, I wished for my old selfishness. I would have gladly slid back into the dream of his impossible mouth. But I could not give myself to it. My cock shrank, becoming a soft coil pursued by Icarus's tongue. I touched his head. "Hey. Thank you."

"I can keep trying."

I disengaged myself, removing my cock from him. Careful not to upset the balance on the chair, I lowered my body until I could look him in the eye. I kissed his forehead. "I know you would. But I can't."

A tear slipped down the side of Icarus's face. "I'm sorry," he whispered. "I'm so sorry."

"Hey," I said. "Hey. You try to get comfortable. I'll go downstairs and get you some more oatmeal."

When I returned with a new bowl, he remained in exactly the

same position, and I realized there was no such thing as comfort in his world any longer.

I returned to the bedroom later with a big saw and a bunch of tools. Icarus flinched at the sight of the equipment. "Relax," I told him. "This isn't for you."

I worked fast and hard, relieved at finally having a way to express my anger. Bookshelves seemed weightless as I shoved them out of the way, rearranging furniture to expose the Eastern wall. One deep breath, and I plunged into it.

In a real house, inside Central City, I could never have cut through a wall with nothing but a handsaw, but this wasn't a real house, and we sure as hell weren't among the privileged. The flimsy wall succumbed to me so easily I wondered how it had stayed standing so long.

"What are you doing?" Icarus gasped as he watched me fling rotten wood and nails into the little piece of yard below our bedroom.

When I was younger, I'd cared about things like that, paying extra to have grass below my window instead of another alley full of discarded things and people. I had changed, and there remained no sign of the flowers I used to grow. The lack of pavement hadn't stopped anyone from using the space as a garbage dump, and I'd have to go down, clean it all out, and cut back the overgrown grass. Any number of disgusting things could be lurking under those long fronds.

The big hole I was making highlighted another benefit of my place. It stood a little taller than the neighbors' places, which I'd wanted so I could divide home and shop. I hadn't even looked through the window in years, but now that I was knocking down the wall, I felt free, and just slightly above it all. It wasn't Central City, but in my youth I'd been able to pretend it was.

"You need more space," I told Icarus. He came to stand beside me, gaping, but I didn't say anything else. I didn't tell him the fantasy I had, that someday those goddamn wings would work and he could fly in and out of our house, swooping off to wherever he wanted through what used to be a wall.

I thought I was old and jaded, but when I remember moments like that with Icarus, it seems like back then I didn't even know what jaded was.

Our new deal required me to ignore Icarus's pain whenever and wherever I could. If I could not actually ignore it, I had to pretend I could.

So, he practiced flying, leaping out that big hole I'd made and screaming when he hit the ground. Sometimes, I thought I could hear his bones thudding into the earth, scraping against each other, even breaking. I got up sometimes, went out the front, and walked around to look into that strip of yard, always expecting to see a busted and twisted Icarus, half-alive and crawling or maybe just staring blankly up at that sky he wanted so badly.

Despite the horrible noises, Icarus didn't manage to kill himself.

I hated it worse when he got up the courage to move his wings. Agonized cries rose with every flap of those feathered titanium monstrosities. Once. Twice. The sounds beginning to fade as Icarus ascended. No matter how I tried not to, I always began to hope right about then. I was never prepared for the little squeal he would give when he could no longer stand the pain.

I learned to turn the music up loud so as not to hear Icarus crashing, Icarus slamming into the side of the house and gasping, Icarus beating his fists into the ground and howling because that hurt, too.

I put on a set of earbuds and gritted my teeth. I did not let myself remember the past, either with a healthy Icarus or before him. I refused to question the work I did now to keep up my payments to the chop man. I just kept the roof over our heads and tried to stay out of his way.

Chapter 4
Fallen Angel Finds His Wings

I didn't like the man sitting across from my computer. In the old days, I wouldn't have answered his query in the first place. There'd been something arrogant about the way he used punctuation, and I hadn't liked the fake, archaic way he'd closed his messages. No one these days wrote, "Yours."

I knew those were arbitrary judgments, but the freedom I used to enjoy allowed me to trust my intuition on subtle signals like that. My new debt reality afforded me the opportunity to confirm that sort of gut feeling in much greater detail than I'd ever wished to—to spend enough time with people to find out why I actually didn't like them.

With this guy, my dislike started with the fastidious care that had gone into his clothing, continued with the way he avoided touching me when I offered my hand, and solidified around the sickly triumph in his eyes as he leaned forward in his chair to say, "You're him, aren't you?"

Whatever it was supposed to mean, I had no patience for that kind of drama. "Him, who?"

"Daedalus. Didn't think you'd be so dense. Where'd you learn how to use this equipment?"

That was bad. He was supposed to be an easy job. He shouldn't know anything about Daedalus. And I liked him even less the more he opened his mouth.

I tried not to let it show on my face. I took a slow, deep breath and raised an eyebrow, aiming my expression toward the threatening side of amused. "You've noticed, I'm sure, that for all of our communications so far we've been utilizing secure, single-use identities. I see no reason to change that custom."

I was talking common courtesy and mutual respect for the reasons neither of us would want to share our identities. Anyone who didn't care about that would be a lot of trouble to me.

If anything, the man's smile broadened. "So, you are Daedalus. I've found you."

"A man who's sitting in my office hoping to get lost shouldn't be worried about what he has or hasn't found."

His expression didn't fade, and the air I breathed suddenly got very sweet and sharp in my nose. Adrenaline pounded through me with every thud of my heart. I'd been waiting for and dreading this moment for a good three decades.

"Don't get up, Daedalus. That wouldn't be wise." He shook his arm as if adjusting his sleeve, and a little pocket pistol popped out and into his hand.

"Would sitting here be any wiser?"

"Central City's on its way already," he said with a shrug. "If you make me shoot you, that just means you won't get far when you try to run. And there are reasons a man might want his legs while they're interrogating him. And especially later, when they drop you in the hold."

A paralyzing agent in the pistol, then. Properly aimed, it could disable the large muscles in the legs, and it sounded like the kind formulated by people who didn't care if the effect turned out permanent or not. Based on the rumors I'd heard, he was telling the truth. A man wanted every means of defense available when they locked him in with thousands of other desperate people in the warrens below Central City. I definitely didn't want to find myself there without the use of my legs.

But what the man had wrong was that, more than anything else, I didn't want to find myself in there at all.

Every heartbeat could have been a mallet pounding in my ears, I was that worked up. I ducked my head like he'd cowed me, and as soon as I saw his shoulders relax, I shoved my desk at him as hard as I could and raced up the stairs. My equipment crashed and shattered in his direction. He cursed and jumped up, aiming that little pistol of his.

I'd hoped to make it up to the bedroom without getting shot. From there, I could jump out the big hole I'd made, and have a chance of getting away. No telling what they'd do to Icarus, but I didn't see how I could help him. The thought made my eyes sting, and for a second I slowed my escape. Shouldn't I let them take me? Icarus would know to stay quiet until he got a chance to jump out that window himself and run for it. If I led them up there now, though, I'd be taking that possibility away from him.

A dart bit into the back of my leg, delivering the wake-up call that freed me from my uncharacteristically selfless daydream. Forget nobility and sacrifice. No way could I stand there and wait for Central City.

I burst into the bedroom. Icarus stood at the space in the wall, his wings spread wide, blocking my way. His hands curled around two cylindrical objects that made him look like an angel clutching a pair of scrolls. "We need to get out of here," I said, slamming the door behind me and locking it. That might hold them for a minute, but I thought I already heard boots stomping through the downstairs. "Central City's here for me, and they're not the kind to let you off the hook for being an innocent bystander."

"Central City? For you?"

"I can't explain. Get out of the way, then get yourself out of here, too." Icarus just stared, like he couldn't make sense of anything I'd said. Before the wings, I would have wished for an evening for a proper goodbye, but considering what we'd been going through, most of what I felt right then was relief. However it went down, I wouldn't have to tiptoe around Icarus anymore. I wouldn't have to wonder if I would get him back, and I wouldn't have to keep selling out for his sake.

I started for Icarus, preparing myself to touch him gently despite my panic. Before I could reach him, the poison dart did its work. My legs collapsed under me, so completely numb that I might as well have fallen on a pile of scrap wood.

I knew I was dead.

Fists pounded on the bedroom door. It shook, the hinges complaining. I glanced from the door to Icarus. I'd been careful before him. Whatever he'd intended, he'd ruined me. He must have seen it in my eyes, because he gave a little cry and ran to me.

"Don't try to *help* me, God damn it!" I snarled at him. "Get out! No sense in them killing both of us."

He seemed so wide-eyed and helpless that my anger melted a little. I touched his arm and pitched my voice softer. "They'll be distracted with me. Jump out the window now, and try not to groan the way you usually do. Don't worry if you're not too mobile. Just find somewhere out of sight and wait until you can't hear anything else. It's probably a good idea to find somewhere else to stay. They might come back here."

He nodded, but didn't otherwise respond to my words. He lifted his hands, and I realized he'd been holding a pair of fat syringes tipped with long, wicked needles. He squeezed his eyes shut and stabbed the first into his thigh, sucking air in through his teeth as he pumped fluid into the thick veins there.

"What the hell are you doing? Cut it out and get out of here!"

Icarus ignored me and stabbed the other needle into his heart. I stared bug-eyed. He grimaced and took that fluid in, too. Then, instead of running to the hole like I wanted him to, he hooked me under the armpits and started hauling me in that direction. I struggled with him, even knowing how I might hurt him. "Forget about me, damn it!"

I screamed the rest of the way to the hole, not caring whether the Central City officials could hear me. Icarus dragged me without noting any of my objections.

Someone kicked the door hard enough that it splintered and buckled. If Icarus was going to escape, he needed to leave now. I reached up and grabbed the back of his head, tugging him down far enough that I could lift my eyes and see his face. "Please," I told him.

The dark eyes that had so captivated me blinked once, slowly. They held a feverishness I didn't like, but also the luster I'd seen the first night. Icarus leaned forward a little more and kissed my forehead. "No," he whispered, stroking his fingers down the side of my face.

I stopped fighting him, even when he pulled me to my feet, settling my back against his chest and wrapping his arms across my torso. I had never really let myself believe that he might feel something for me. I had never been worthy of that from him—even moments ago, I'd been ready to abandon him to Central City.

The door split in two, and a pistol came in, followed by a large man. Icarus's arms tightened around me. He coiled low, taking my body with him, then leapt into the air accompanied by a cry. But I was the one who screamed, the beat of his wings ripping through me as if they were my own.

More shots rang out. They must have hit my legs. I didn't feel anything, but I saw something drip from my shoe.

Above and behind me, Icarus flapped his wings slowly, power-fully, and steadily, lifting our double weight with alarming speed. We rose above the Central City police vans parked in front of my home. Men, growing smaller, talked on radios and pointed upward.

Ice ran through my veins, but I could not remain concerned when we rose above the dilapidated roofs of my building and the neigh-bors'. Finally, we were high enough to see the pattern of the streets, far enough away from the specifics that the brutal design of it all made a cold kind of sense. Central City's spires rose in the middle and ev-erything fell from there, shadow cities produced as part of the great city's half-life, going on into the infinite distance, but possessing less and less of its radiant glory.

"How are you doing this?" I shouted. I wasn't sure if Icarus could hear me over the whoosh of his enormous wings. "I thought you couldn't actually fly."

He gave me a squeeze. "Adrenaline and painkillers," he shouted back into my ear. "Lots of them." He smiled beatifically, as if he'd just declared his love.

I had never thought of Icarus as having much strength, but now his hold on me was the only thing preventing me from falling to my death. I closed my eyes against what waited for us below and allowed his arms around me to be my only reality.

He grunted with effort. His laboring wings lifted us in a slow and straining spiral, higher and higher. The air thinned. His sweat soaked through my clothes, and the elevation's cold air plastered the clammy garments against my body and made me shiver.

Solid ground was the farthest thing from my mind. My eyes snapped open in shock when the backs of my hands bumped against a surface, and Icarus sighed, maneuvered, and set us down.

He did not collapse as I expected. Instead, I was the one who fell. My legs still didn't work. Bullets had grazed my skin in several places. My jeans clung stickily to the holes. I winced and loosened them, wondering if I wanted to find out how much they hurt.

Icarus stood above me. Pain burned in his eyes, but his face glowed.

The world around me glittered, blinding. I blinked and tried to catch my bearings. "Where are we?"

"The Spire. It's a thousand feet higher than the Skywalk." He dropped to his knees beside me, winding one arm around the back of my neck. "You can see that restaurant I told you about from here." He directed my head, but everything looked the same to me—glass and reflected sun.

"We're in Central City?" My head snapped frantically from left to right. "Won't they send someone after us?" Surely, we couldn't be safe up there.

Icarus smiled, his face shining more than the city below. "City regulations prohibit motor vehicles in the sky. The angel-men don't want to deal with police. They want to be free, and they've got the resources to reserve a space all to themselves." His fingers trailed over my skin. "I'm one of them now. I've got the wings to prove it."

I knew better. No one in Central City had ever suffered for wings the way that Icarus had. But I didn't want to spoil his happiness. I kept my mouth shut and kissed him.

He responded with a fire I'd never felt from him before, hands delving under my clothes, tongue driving into my mouth. "You gave this to me," he said against my lips. I accepted his adoration, putting his recent misery out of my mind. He felt good. I closed my eyes, reached around him, and, for the first time, stroked the feathers of his wings. Soft and cold, they sliced my fingertips like the edge of a sheet of paper. My breath caught in my lungs. He seemed so fragile to me. Something that hurt me had to hurt him, too.

But Icarus moaned. "You reach right inside me when you do that."

157

Watching his face, I flattened one hand against his wing, its titanium ridges pressing firmly into my palm. Icarus sighed, wrapped me in his body, and kicked off from the roof, taking us into a backward dive.

I screamed, struggling mindlessly in his grasp even though I knew that victory would mean my death. Icarus held on, crooning to me within the cocoon of his wings. Fear erased my mind, and all I could do was breathe and wait, clutched against the winged man's chest, wondering what we were to each other.

Then Icarus unfurled his wings with a bracing snap, and we stopped diving, rising sharply on a gust of wind that took us higher than the most exclusive penthouses reserved for the most exclusive denizens of Central City. He started touching me again, one arm securing me while the other fiddled with my pants.

"What are you—"

Icarus just smiled. He couldn't hear me, and what I would have said didn't matter anyway. He loosened my pants from my waist, then used his toes to push and pull them down my legs. Freed from me, they floated and snapped in the various air currents around us, moving slower than I would have expected, but always downward.

My boxers got the same treatment, and Icarus took my hard cock in his hand. I reached around to grip his ass, to start opening him up, but he wriggled it out of my grasp and slid his hands around to my ass instead. I jumped, surprised. Icarus had never touched me there before.

His wings beat in a steady pulse as his hands maneuvered me into position. He hung in the air, facing the city below, and hooked my legs up over his shoulders. I didn't have the leverage or the sensation to move them away from where he placed them. I clung to his neck with my arms, aware that my entire weight now dangled from his upper body.

Icarus slid his fingers into his mouth, then moved the moisture to my ass. Though they'd just come from a warm place, they'd chilled by the time they touched the ring of muscle there. I shivered when he slipped one inside. Icarus leaned forward and kissed me as he probed me. My leg muscles would probably have complained if I could have felt them—I was never very flexible.

For all my fantasies about Icarus, and all my lust, I'd never thought about taking him in. But at that moment, rushing through a sky that seemed to belong to him, it seemed only natural that I should belong to him, too.

I wasn't quite ready for him when he fitted his cock to my ass, but I didn't want to make him wait. He held me by the shoulders and hunched his abs up to press into my ass. The display of strength would have amazed me if I hadn't been so distracted by the effort of receiving him. I didn't think I could take it, and I would have jumped away if I hadn't been forced to hold on. Every new bit of territory he claimed overwhelmed me. Every time his cock thrust deeper, I didn't think I could accept it. I didn't know how to open up for him.

But Icarus didn't pull back, and I didn't make him. With every beat of his wings and every tightening of the large muscles along his waist, his cock lodged a little deeper. I didn't realize it at first, but by the time his balls made contact with my ass, fitting his cock into me to the root, I realized I'd never been so hard. My own cock ached and wept, and my balls had drawn up tight against my skin like I was about to come.

Icarus grabbed my ass and pulled me even closer, shoving the final bit of his cock inside me, as far as it would go. And suddenly, the whole thing changed, and I wanted more of him and harder and faster. I couldn't make my knees bend, couldn't drive myself up and down on his cock. I tried to use my arms to swing myself, but Icarus shook his head and fucked me himself. The muscles in his arms corded as he slid me back and forth in time with the flapping of his wings.

I squeezed his neck tightly at first, but the pleasure made me want to arch my back. Eventually, I let go, my torso swinging freely in the air below him, trusting myself entirely to Icarus's hands and cock to hold me up as he flew us higher, and ever higher.

Blood rushed to my head. With me dangling that way, he'd had to stop thrusting, but just the sensation of him filling me began to feel unbearably intense. I'd closed my eyes at some point, and when I opened them, I went immediately dizzy. We'd flown higher than I could comprehend. I gasped. The air couldn't sustain me. I couldn't understand how Icarus's wings could even find purchase in such a thin world.

No matter what difficulties I perceived, nothing slowed his flying or eased the grip of his hands. He groaned above me, and suddenly our angle changed wildly. My head spun as I flipped and twisted on his cock. Then I screamed as my cock began to shoot, my seed freezing almost instantly in the chill upper atmosphere, and the pleasure splitting my head apart as I gasped for air and could not get enough.

Icarus gripped my ass hard enough to hurt. He emptied himself inside me, his cock's pulsing making it feel even larger inside my stretched asshole.

I felt absolutely free. I crunched up toward Icarus for one delirious, delicious kiss. We laughed into each other's mouths.

Then I ran my hand over my thigh and noticed it was wet. I pulled away from Icarus's kiss and found a stream of blood running down my numb leg, dripping off his wing and onto me. Far too much blood.

The mood hadn't yet left him. No strain showed in his face. Though I knew at that instant that he was dead, Icarus did not realize it until after we reached the ground.

We touched down on the outskirts of nowhere, far from where I'd lived most of my life, and far from anything either of us had ever known. I spent the next two days holding him. The wounds from the chop man never again stopped bleeding, no matter how I tried to stop them up.

He'd gotten the drugs from the chop man, after an agonizing limped journey one day while I was working. The chop man told him he would probably only ever manage to fly once, but that didn't stop Icarus. I couldn't bear to ask how he paid the man.

Not long after he told me that, after we left the paradise we'd found in the upper sky, Icarus went away and never returned. His eyes never focused on me, and he never again reached out to touch me.

I tried to keep my legs from getting infected. A jagged, piercing feeling slowly returned to them. Sensation would shoot down one leg or the other at odd moments, interspersed with deadness. I could move them, and I could walk, but it was impossible to accomplish either feat precisely. I did not let this trouble me while I breathed, sweated, and sighed with Icarus.

I was hungry, thirsty, and lost when I closed his eyes for the last time. Sliding out from under him with a lot of help from my hands, I rose shakily to my feet. Had I loved him? I thought love was supposed to be a nobler emotion, so much less selfish. I thought love was about giving not taking, about asking what I could do rather than what would be done for me.

I wanted to kick those wings, which dwarfed his body so utterly. I wanted to tear them off and feed those titanium rods to the chop man slice by bloody slice. It didn't matter that they had made Icarus happy. They still looked alive, while the rest of him had shriveled.

I buried him. I found a piece of scrap that served as a shovel, and I found an alley no one had bothered to pave. I couldn't dig deep enough to get the wings all the way underground, so feathers became his gravestone, poking up from the disturbed earth on either side of him.

If you enjoyed this story, you can sign up for a free membership at
ForbiddenFiction and discuss it with other readers
and the author at the *Icarus Bleeds* story page
at http://forbiddenfiction.com/library/story/AL1-1.000140.

Elf Esteem

Nobilis Reed

A few years ago, Nobilis Reed decided to start sharing the naughty little stories he scribbled out in hidden notebooks. To his surprise, people actually liked them! Now, he can't stop. The poor man is addicted. His wife, teenage children, and even the cats just look on this wretch of a man and shake their heads. The best that can be hoped for is to just make him as comfortable as his condition will allow. Symptoms include two novels, several novellas, numerous short stories, and the longest-running erotica podcast on Earth. His website is at www.nobiliserotica.com.

Elf Esteem

I live alone, so hearing the sound of my computer booting up in the middle of the night is a little surreal. Add that to the fact I hadn't slept for at least twenty-four hours and you can understand why I wasn't in a completely normal state of mind. I put on some panties and a tee shirt so I'd be at least a little decent, and crept down the stairs.

When I saw my computer mouse moving around with nobody sitting in front of it, I was pretty sure I was either dreaming or hallucinating. When I got a little closer, and spotted the little creature pushing it about, I blinked, shook my head, and looked again.

I had a pretty good vantage point from the stairs, looking straight down at the coffee table where my keyboard and mouse sat next to an empty pizza box and the tablet computer I use when out of the house. Right there, both hands on the mouse, was an honest-to-god fairy, about six inches tall. She had pale skin, long hair that was so blonde it was yellow, and a dress that looked like it might have been made out of leaves. I sat down on the steps, rubbed my eyes, and looked again. Still there.

What the hell did a fairy want with my computer?

I looked up at my big HD screen on the wall. It was easy to see what she was bringing up, even from across the room.

Porn. She went straight into my bookmarks folder, down to the one marked "macramé," and pulled up one of my old favorites. "Furry Lady dot com" splashed across my screen. My login and password were already filled in and I watched in stunned silence as she entered the site and started browsing through the available videos.

I stormed down the steps and stood in front of her.

"Excuse me? What do you think you're doing?"

I'm used to making an impression when I confront someone, especially by surprise. I'm not short, and I'm not small. Maybe the impact was lessened a bit by the fact that my sizable tits were unrestrained by anything resembling a bra, but I was mad and the thought hadn't occurred to me to put on a robe.

"Oh!" Her voice was incredibly high-pitched. "Excuse me!" She had an odd accent, a cross between Scottish and Welsh, and sounded more surprised than scared. "I thought you'd be sleeping. I'll just be on my way, go ahead, don't mind me." She flew up into the air, did a quick loop-the-loop, and flitted backwards toward the kitchen area. She was flapping her little blue butterfly wings as fast as she could, but she was about as fast as a butterfly, too. Not very.

I spotted the open window behind her, ran across the room and slammed it shut.

"So you're the one who's been cutting holes in my screens!"

"Sorry!" She backed away again, landing on the back of my couch. "I didn't mean to rile ye. I was just curious about all the pretty lasses."

I slapped my forehead and blinked.

"What the fuck am I doing. I'm standing here shouting at a fairy." I sat down at my dining table and tried to get my head together. It didn't feel like a dream and I hadn't taken anything to make me hallucinate. I began to doubt my sanity.

There was a -thunk- on the table next to me, followed by a gently crinkling pop and a hiss. I looked up. There was a beer, freshly opened, a wisp of condensation floating from the mouth. Standing next to it was the fairy, with an apologetic smile on her face. Up close, I saw her dress wasn't made of the leaves and bark I originally thought, but was carefully folded out of crisp paper money. She was slim and athletic in build, like a dancer or a fencer.

"Thanks," I said, bringing the cold bottle to my lips.

"You're welcome!" I took a swallow then pulled it away with a grimace.

"Shit." I stood up, emptied the beer into the sink and dropped the bottle into the recycling.

"What's the matter?"

"It's an India pale ale. Those were for my ex."

"You miss her fiercely," said the fairy.

"Gee, how'd you guess?"

"You drank a hogshead o' beer and watched porn until the wee hours o' the night," she said, completely missing my sarcasm.

"So you're a peeping Tom, as well as a trespasser." Getting off the subject of Paula felt like a very good idea.

She scratched her head and shrugged. "I guess I am." She didn't seem in any way apologetic.

"Why?" I asked. "The wee folk aren't known for interest in computers."

"Just curious. I saw what you were watching. I wanted to see more."

"After six hours?"

"Well, that *was* three weeks ago, ye ken."

"Wait a minute...I've replaced that screen three times since them. How often have you been coming in and using my computer?"

"Every night." There was no shame in her voice, no blush to her pale complexion. She was totally unrepentant. "It would have been easier if you'd leave the chimney flue open once in a while."

"Shit."

"It's not as good as a real tumble, though," said the fairy, glancing over her shoulder at the screen.

"No, it's not."

"So why haven't you found another playmate? You're a fair lass! You've got hair the color o' roses, a bounteous bosom and plentiful posterior, and you have freckles enough for three leopards."

I groaned and shook my head. I definitely didn't need those last few attributes highlighted, and my hair color came out of a bottle.

"I'll never find anyone like Paula. What we had was special. You wouldn't understand."

"I'm smart," she said. "Probably the smartest fairy around here. Sharp enough to figure out yon computer. I'll wager I ken."

"In a small town like this, it's hard enough finding another dyke, much less one I can connect with like I did with her. Add to that..."

"That you like getting tied up?"

I scowled.

"I've seen you watch porn, and I know what you have in the box under the bed. I know what you like."

"Don't remind me."

"You're angry at me."

"Yes! Of course I'm angry at you! You broke into my house! Invaded my privacy! I think I have a right to be angry."

"Maybe I could help you relax?" She cocked her head to one side and gave me a sexy smile.

I laughed.

"You? You want to top *me*? Kiddo, I'm twenty-two stone. If I sat on you, I'd probably squash you flat."

"I'm not a kid. I'm a hundred and eighty years old. And I'm stronger than I look."

"I guess you'd have to be to get a beer out of the pantry. But being a top is about more than just what you see in porn. There's a relationship there. Trust. A common sense of purpose. How can I trust you?" I couldn't believe I was having this conversation with a fairy.

"You mortals. Always so afraid. And you think we're silly. Why not just try it and see? What have you got to lose?"

"If there's an emergency, I need to know you can get me free in a hurry, for one thing."

"That's fair. Go get a rope."

"You're going to cut it?"

"You'll see."

I went to the bedroom and got a big thick one, and dumped it onto the dining room table. She picked up the end and held it out to me.

"Tie a few loops around your thigh, as tight as you can."

I sat down at the dining room table and did as she said. I wasn't a rigger by any stretch of the imagination, but I had picked up a few tricks. I made several loops, knotting them together on each wrapping, to make a decorative sheath running halfway down my thigh.

"Ready?" she asked.

"Go for it." I leaned back in my chair.

She jumped from her spot on the table and flew down onto my thigh. She hardly weighed anything. When she shook her behind, glittery dust fell from her wings and the knots were gone. They hadn't broken or snapped, the ropes hadn't been cut or shredded, the knots were just *gone*. The rope hung from my thigh as if I'd just laid it there.

She turned and looked up at me, with her chin held up and fists propped on her hips.

"Okay," I said, becoming even more convinced I'd come unhinged. "I guess you can handle that part." I picked up the coil of rope and laid it back on the table.

"Anything else on your mind? Any other reservations?" she asked.

"I guess I'm just having trouble imagining how it would work. You're so small."

"That doesn't sound like a reason not to try it. That sounds like a reason to go for it."

"I think I at least need to know your name."

"'Mistress' will suffice."

I shrugged. "I guess."

"So is it a deal? Do you promise to do as I say, until you say your safeword?"

"Okay, as long as you don't gag me. I don't like being gagged."

"I won't put anything in your mouth," she said, with a sparkle in her eye. "Do you promise?"

"Yes."

Her face lit up with a broad smile, and she clapped her hands together.

"Marvelous! Bring your toy box out to the living room."

I got up from my chair, went to the bedroom where the big wooden box of rope and other toys was stored, and met her out where the computer was still running.

"Set them down here on the table, and push it out of the way. We're going to do this right on the floor." I did as she said, and stood in the middle of the room.

"Good! You're an obedient creature, I see." She fluttered around me then sat on the table I'd pushed aside. "Take off your clothes." When I opened my mouth to say something, she raised her hand and waggled a finger at me. "And don't speak unless it's to say your safeword!"

I nodded. I did not yet feel the warm excitement playing bondage games with my ex brought, but we had only gotten started. I figured I could play along until it either happened, or it was clear it wasn't going to. Mostly, I was curious about how she was going to manage it. Fairy dust or not, she just didn't seem to have the gravitas to be a real top.

Then again, she had gotten me to shut up. Paula had never managed that.

While I was stripping down, she sorted through my rope collection and set pieces aside. Even the biggest coils weren't too heavy for her, but several of them were awkward for her to handle. She piled those to one side. The ones she picked out were either thin, or short. These she tied knots in, occasionally giving me an appraising glance. I started to wonder what she had in store for me.

When I was naked, she had me sit in the middle of the floor, and gave me two pieces tied-off in loops about eight inches in diameter, which went loosely over my thighs. Then she handed me one of the smallest ropes in the collection. It was hardly more than a scrap, just a foot long or so and only four millimeters in diameter. She had me use it to tie my big toes together. The black twist contrasted with my pale skin in a way that always looked attractive to me, which was why all the rope in my collection was black.

Next came a yard-long piece of rope with a hard, fixed loop on one end, and a slip-knot loop on the other. The fixed loop went over my head, with the end trailing down my back.

At her command I bent forward, raised my knees, and slipped my arms down through the loops on my thighs, so that my shoulders and knees touched. She then moved behind me and had me put my hands through a loop of rope that ran through the slip knot, and tug it tight.

She'd tied the loops at just the right length to bind without cutting off my circulation. I wanted to ask how she had gotten them so perfect without having to measure, but I didn't want to break the atmosphere I felt building around us.

One moment I was completely free to move, and a few seconds later I was securely bound from knees to wrists. I took a deep breath-- or at least, as deep a breath as I could take, bent over the way I was— and took stock.

I wasn't completely immobilized, but all I could really do was squirm. I could shuffle around a little on my heels and my butt. As

I realized just how limited I was, I felt that shivering realization that yes, I was stuck, and yes, I really was at her mercy.

"There you go," she said. "Anything binding too much? Any problems?" She walked around me, tugging at the ropes to check the knots.

I shook my head.

"Excellent. You're doing quite well. Now do you believe this will work?"

I nodded.

"You may speak, if you like."

"Thank you, Mistress."

She clapped her hands and hopped into the air and hovered.

"Oh, wonderful! I've got a mortal subbie. We are going to have so much fun!" The gesture would have broken the mood if it weren't for the devilish look in her eye.

She stepped over my feet, into the space between my legs, under my torso. Her tiny hands caressed my breasts, making slow circles on the flesh hanging above her. My nipples stiffened, but she teased me, coming closer and closer but never quite touching.

"These are marvelous!" She said. "Oh, I could play with these all night." She looked up at me, that scary-cute smile broadening. "What do you think of that idea?"

"Please, mistress. I would like more than that."

"Oh, so you're a greedy wench, are you? Here we went to all the trouble to get you tied up and you want more?" she asked, still stroking and kneading my too-long neglected flesh.

"Yes. I am."

"Well then..." She flitted up to the toy box and pulled out the homemade nipple clamps. I made them myself, just a pair of springy clothespins with some twine strung between them. They hadn't been attached to me in years. With a bit of old clothesline looped over one shoulder, she flitted back to where she had been. She slapped each nipple lightly to get it good and hard, then squeezed the arms of a clothespin between both hands to get it to open and clamp down. When both were in place, she tugged lightly on the string, looking up into my face.

I didn't remember the sensation being that strong. They squeezed hard, and I winced with each tug on the string. It wasn't quite enough to make me cry out, but it was definitely having an effect.

She giggled and looped the clothesline over the string, causing more tugs on the clothespins.

"Now I want you to keep these here," she said. "I like the pink color they bring to your nipples. Such a lovely shade! It would be a shame to lose it."

"Yes, mistress."

She reached up and patted me on the cheek.

"That's the right attitude!" Then she shivered with glee and bent down on her hands and knees, pushing the clothesline down under my butt. Her wings fluttered briefly against my sex and I felt a tingle run up my spine.

I gasped, making her giggle again. I whimpered when she stopped.

"Aww, don't worry my pet. We'll be back there before too long." She zipped out and around behind me, and I craned my head to look over my shoulder. She fished the rope out from underneath me, making the soft cotton rub against me as it went.

"Head back," she said. "Look up at the ceiling." I obeyed, and there were more tugs on the clothespins, along with new ones on my hair. She was tying the ends to my ponytail, carefully arranging the clothesline to run between my labia, on either side of my clit. I could feel the soft cotton sheath of the ropes between the cheeks of my ass. My head wasn't pulled back at an extreme angle, but I wouldn't be able to move much without pulling off at least one of the clothespins, and I didn't want to do that.

Huh.

I didn't want to pull off the clothespins. I thought the feeling of not wanting to disappoint was something special for Paula, something that came from being in love with her, part of our special relationship.

The relationship that turned out not to be so special after all.

It felt good, there, the same as always. In fact, it was a little stronger than usual. The feeling was almost as strong as the first time Paula and I tried out that hunk of clothesline and discovered just how much I liked being tied up. A painful tug on my nipples told me I was letting my head fall too far forward. I pulled back, lifting my gaze from the floor.

There was a new image on the computer. My mistress had flown over to the keyboard and brought up a different site.

A bondage site, one I wasn't familiar with. This wasn't something from my usual bookmarks. She signed in, created a login and password, and picked out a video, obviously quite familiar with the process.

"Wait!" I exclaimed, "That's my credit card number!" I straightened up, which brought my head forward, which in turn yanked one of the clothespins off. A little "eep" escaped my lips both from the shock of the release, the rope rubbing against my clit, and the realization I had disobeyed two of my new mistress's commands.

She turned and put her little hands on her hips, and flew up so she was silhouetted against the screen. She clicked her tongue and shook her head.

"There you go, undoing all my hard work." She flitted down beneath me and put the clothespin back in place. "This definitely requires a response, don't you think so?"

I started to speak, and stopped myself. I nodded. The movement rubbed the rope against my clit some more and tugged the clothespins on my nipples; I gasped in pleasure.

She laughed and flew back to the toy box, clearing my field of view so I could see the video. The girl on the screen was getting tied to a spider web made of heavy chains, hanging upside-down with loops of rope all over her body. She had a really nice figure, soft boobs and well-padded thighs that took a dramatic imprint of the ropes against her body.

"What do you think?" she said, pulling a Ping-Pong paddle out of the box and giving it a few practice swings.

I nodded again, feeling a tingle of anticipation come to my ass. Once again, the rope transferred the movement to my nipples and clit, and I had to stifle a moan.

"Okay, now get on your knees," she said, as she flew over my back and behind me.

I scooched my feet in and rolled forward, landing clumsily on my knees. The movement pushed my forehead against the carpet, and made the ropes shift once again. The position was marvelously humbling, especially given the size of my mistress.

The experience was different from my sessions with Paula, I realized. She spent a lot of energy trying to out-butch me, metaphorically climbing on top, rather than giving me the challenge of dropping down and relaxing into the bottom role. With my new mistress, there was no question of who was stronger or tougher. I was. And it didn't matter; she was the top and that was all there was to it. There was no need to dominate physically, because she had the confidence and charm to make me do all the work.

"What do you think, would twenty strokes be enough?" she asked from behind me.

I couldn't turn my head to see, so I just nodded.

"Count 'em," she said, and the first blow landed on my ass. The paddle had a nubby rubber surface that did nothing to cushion the blow. What's more, even in the fairies' tiny hands, it landed with a definite bite.

"One," I said, my voice already becoming breathy and choked. Another stroke landed, on the other ass cheek. "Two." The pain was sharp and tingly, spreading warmth over my posterior as the blood rose to the surface. I knew I would already be turning red.

I could no longer see the video. There was a slapping noise coming from it, sounding like a flogger of some kind, and murmurs of pain and ecstasy. The sub had been gagged. I wished my mistress had gagged me; it was so much harder to stay quiet, to limit myself to counting off the numbers, without it.

I concentrated on counting and maintaining my composure. My world narrowed to just those numbers and the stinging slap of the paddle against my ass. Nothing else existed, nothing else mattered, nothing else could intrude. Work, family, and even the mourning of my relationship with Paula fell away.

After the last blow landed, I felt a gentle touch on my rump.

"Now then, feeling better?"

"Uh-huh."

"You can talk now, if you like."

"Thank you, mistress."

She walked around to my face, pushed up against the carpet, and kissed my cheek.

"I think you're due for a reward."

"Thank you, mistress."

I heard her wings flutter, but I wasn't paying attention to where she was anymore, or what she was doing. I was too far gone, too deep into the experience to care. When I felt her fiddling with the ropes running between my pussy lips, I didn't think, 'What is she doing?' I just accepted it. It was happening, it felt good, and that's all that mattered.

Something small, round, and hard nestled between the ropes and my inner lips, and then it started to buzz. As the sensation built, I recognized it as the variable-speed vibrating egg Paula surprised me with a year or so before. We left it in the bottom of the toy box after the first few tries because it seemed too weak, but placed where it was, on the surface instead of down inside, it was much more intense. I moaned out loud, desperate to arch my back, but every movement tugged on my nipples, reminding me to keep still. The effect increased the tension in my muscles, as I held myself as still as I could.

With the ropes holding it in place, my mistress shifted her attention to my clit. The ropes still ran on either side, and as I dealt with the effects of the vibrator, they rubbed against it in slight, uneven strokes. Then I felt her hands on it, kneading and caressing, far more delicate than even a tongue could be. The contrast between the heaviness of the ropes and the feather-light touch of her hands was like nothing I'd felt before. I struggled against the urgent need to thrash against my bonds.

Both clothespins popped off at once as I finally let go, spasms rocking my body so hard I thought I might fall over. I could hear my mistress's exultant, bubbly laughter all through it. When I was finally able to open my eyes again, I was greeted by the sight of a naked fairy standing about a foot in front of my face, hands on hips, dripping wet. I fought hard to stifle a chuckle but a bit of it got out.

"Will you just look at me?" she said. "You got me all wet."

"I'm sorry, mistress," I said, without much sincerity.

"I think you need to clean me off."

"Yes, mistress." I tried to slip back into the submissive role but it wasn't easy.

She walked over to my mouth and slapped my upper lip.

"Tongue," she said.

I stuck out my tongue. She used it like a bath towel, guiding it over her tiny body, while she ooh-ed and ah-ed and mm-ed. It was hard to identify which body parts I was licking, everything was so tiny and universally wet. After a few big slurps, I felt one leg swing over my tongue, and she began rubbing against it. Based on the glimpses I could see down below my nose, she seemed to be humping the side, so I made it as hard and flat as I could, which wasn't an easy task.

She didn't complain. After a minute or so of humping, she let out a long, shrill cry and slumped against my face.

"My my, that was fun," she said breathlessly. It only took a few seconds to catch her breath. "There now, don't you feel better?"

"Yes, I think I do," I said. "Thank you. Though I think my hands are starting to go numb."

"Ah, yes. Let's get you out of all that." She flew over me and suddenly I was free. The ropes fell away.

I sat back and shook the blood back into my hands, and checked my body for marks. There were distinct impressions on my wrists, and somewhat lighter ones on my shoulders and thighs. They stung a little, but it was more of a nice memory than anything unpleasant.

I stood and shut off the computer. There was a bit of a wet spot on the carpet, but it wasn't anything that hadn't happened before. I knew how to clean it up. The thing I wanted to clean first was myself. "I'm going to take a shower," I said. "Care to wash my back?"

In legend, fairies are known to be fickle creatures, easily distracted and fond of leaving humans puzzled whenever we think we've figured them out. This proved to be true for my visitor as well. I never saw her again after that night. I missed her for a while, but when I realized she wasn't coming back, I put myself together, and posted a message on my favorite social fetish site.

"Lesbian bondage slut seeks top. Age, weight, height unimportant."

If you enjoyed this story, you can sign up for a free membership at
ForbiddenFiction and discuss it with other readers
and the author at the *Elf Esteem* story page
at http://forbiddenfiction.com/library/story/NR1-1.000118.

About the Publisher

ForbiddenFiction.com is a publisher devoted to writing that breaks the boundaries of original erotic fiction. Our stories combine intense sexuality with quality writing. Stories at ForbiddenFiction.com not only arouse readers through sensations, but also engage them emotionally and mentally through storytelling as well-crafted as the sex is hot.

ForbiddenFiction.com is also designed to be a social reading environment. You'll have fun even if just reading the latest post each day, yet you will have the chance for so much more. Readers and authors can be part of ongoing discussions of specific works and individual authors as well as more general topics.

Sign up for a FREE Membership today at ForbiddenFiction.com

www.ingramcontent.com/pod-product-compliance
Lightning Source LLC
Chambersburg PA
CBHW060109260626
47160CB00005B/1843